THE BETTERTON
FRACTURE

W. MARSHALL HARVEY

Order this book online at www.trafford.com
or email orders@trafford.com

Most Trafford titles are also available at major online book retailers.

Print information available on the last page.

ISBN: 978-1-6987-0127-1 (sc)
ISBN: 978-1-6987-0126-4 (hc)
ISBN: 978-1-6987-0128-8 (e)

Library of Congress Control Number: 2020910152

Illustrations by: Sandra C. Pouncey

Author's Photo Credit: Hattie Grace Summers

Trafford rev. 06/04/2020

www.trafford.com
North America & international
toll-free: 1 888 232 4444 (USA & Canada)
fax: 812 355 4082

CONTENTS

To my family, and to my husband, Christopher Harvey.
You all make everyday life the stuff of dreams.

ACKNOWLEDGMENTS

I would like to thank Katie Johns, Samantha Roberts, Sandra Pouncey, Joyce Bixler, Judy Venters, and Regina Derrick for their invaluable time, thorough feedback, and pertinent suggestions. I am profoundly appreciative that you shared your discerning viewpoints with me.

1

ADDISON

Knowing how to put up a fight can be difficult for people who have never so much as made an effort at being unfriendly. In this town, people are used to blessing sneezes, waving through car windows, and holding doors for perfect strangers if you were to ever encounter one. It's sort of the North Carolina way, I guess. In my family, conflict has always been handled behind closed doors and in civil voices. It is no wonder that confronting despicable acts of intimidation has felt so unsettling. We all know that such things cannot be excused or allowed to go unanswered.

But it isn't simple for the lamb to turn and face the wolf.

Sharron looks shaken as she ties her hair back tonight. She's not the nervous sort, but right now her jaw is clenched so tightly that I bet it could crush a stone. The town council of Betterton will be meeting later to discuss the war, though I fear any directives coming from this council will be about as useful as a teardrop in a wildfire.

I call my mother Sharron because that is what everyone else calls her. I only say "Mama" by mistake when I am scared or not paying close attention to how my thoughts come out in words, which is rare. Growing up in the Gain household, one learns to properly navigate the English language. Sometimes Sharron speaks as if she were of another age when words were chosen deliberately to enhance meaning instead of haphazardly to express thoughts.

She likes to tie her hair back like that so nobody can see how shiny and beautiful it is. She does not care to wear makeup or stand out at all. Many women go out of their way to adorn themselves and plaster their faces with color. Not Sharron Gain. She is perfectly content to blend in with her surroundings. Being present but unseen is her preference. She does, however, wear an elegant, sweet scent that lingers in the air as she drifts from one space to another. She's worn it as long as I can remember. You have to get very close to appreciate the real spice of it, though she is not likely to allow that to happen. And if you happen to collide with her under the wrong circumstance, she can be quite formidable. Sometimes I think of her as a razor hidden in blades of grass.

This would be my favorite part of a normal night. I would be getting freshly showered and comfortably into my silk pajamas, well-fed, tired, and ready to bid the day goodbye. Especially in September when there's a chill in the air. Sharron would be combing the long blond strands of her mane as diligently and delicately as an artist taking great care to do justice to their work. We would watch some reality TV until I heard, "Addison, hon, time for bed." Then I would stumble bleary-eyed down the hall where I could collapse onto my perfectly plush mattress, lie my head along the cool surface of my firm pillow, and descend willfully into a dreamy abyss.

Not tonight. Tonight the war spills over. There will be nothing dreamy about this evening. Sharron and I have always lived in this little town in North Carolina. It's about forty miles north of Wilmington, as the crow flies. Betterton. Don't let the name fool you. It's not a bad place to be planted, but once you flower, it is best to catch the wind to greener pastures. Recently it has become a hard place to be. Not wonderful, not unlivable. Just hard.

The town hasn't always been like this. When I was a little girl, I remember everybody being very happy—damned near chipper all of the time. There were more people then. Sharron and I used to spend Saturdays walking up Main Street up to Mason's Drug to get me an ice cream and her a cherry Coke.

Most Saturdays we would walk back up Main Street and cross behind town hall to find respite in Glenn W. Watson Park, named for the late civil rights leader who had worked to integrate schools in Betterton. This time of year we would most likely be accompanied by a brisk wind and the sound of pecan shells crunching against the sidewalk as people pass by. Benton, a gentleman from our church with Down's Syndrome, would usually be out and about on a sunny day, though he didn't care much for the clear weather. Benton is after two things in the world: members of his church and his phone. He has a warming smile that I swear could calm a rough sea. He is the sort of fellow that you make a point of speaking to—if for no other reason than to make your day a little less heavy.

It was easy to get lost in your own thoughts in the park. There were a few swings and monkey bars to occupy the little ones, but the sun and the trees were the main event. Beautiful sweetgums, hickories, and red maples in persistent undulation with the wind and the air and the butterflies. I recall the cold ice cream on my lips contrasting with the feeling of the sun blanketing my shoulders. Sundays I always had to wear a sweater or shawl to cover up my shoulders for services at the Baptist church. But Saturdays were my salvation. That was the one day of the week when everyone in town willingly suspended all need of piety or the need to be proper. It was as if the day itself could vanquish my worries like hot soap and water could purify a face and make it new again. Just me and Sharron and the ice cream and the sun and the trees. I think back on those days with a somber smile and a somewhat frustrated lamentation.

There isn't much else to do in town besides killing time and enjoying good weather. We have a diner and a bowling alley across from Betterton Senior High, but only unwed baby boomers and creepy old men hang out there. Nichol's Drive-In was fine, but Sharron is not exactly hemorrhaging money. Being a secretary at the Muldune Cotton and Fiber Mill doesn't, as they so eloquently say in these parts, put you too high on the hog. In fact, if not for whatever she inherited from her parents, we'd be close to destitute. Still, we are happy, she and I. In another place Sharron would be a CEO, the boss, a force to be reckoned with. She is singularly the most well-spoken, intelligent woman I have had the pleasure of calling a role model. Meanwhile, whoever my dad was had been long gone since before memories required pictures.

When I was a little girl, the town was full of life. Full of light. All smiles, and "How you doin'?" and people calling each other brother, sugar, and hon. Then, when I was in about the fourth grade, the great housing crash happened. Betterton was not spared. People lost houses and had to move away. Mr. Fetter had a tough time keeping up with his tab at Dixie Hardware and Feed. Even the ice cream and cherry Coke disappeared from my Saturdays in the park.

The great cataclysm came when the mill closed. The speed of the change was dizzying. It seemed like I took a breath one day, and as quickly as I exhaled, the whole mill village in the northeast part of town was hollow. I'd say empty, but the word *empty* feels too . . . too clean. Too neat and tidy. A water glass or an oak cabinet can be empty. Nothing wrong or unsettling there. But *hollow* means something's been taken. Like there used to be something meaningful or even joyful there. Like it had a heart, which beats no longer. Like all that remains is a lifeless cavity from which life once emanated but now only silence/death echoes in the wind. *Hollow.*

The village was constructed to house the mill workers. It was built in closely lined blocks of numbered streets and avenues. Little houses lined up side by side like a fifties rerun. Green ones, white ones, blue ones. All with trimmed yards and sparkling windows. At least you could say the people took great pride and care in where they lived. There were about fifty or so still there, but without the showroom-new facade. The structures now stand like tombstones memorializing a life that was but is no more, presided over by a hollow industrial mausoleum.

Like the rest of America, Betterton survived the financial mess. The Price and Fetter Farms still raise soy, corn, and tobacco. The Decello family boasts a head of livestock that could rival any farm in all of the Carolinas. The three agricultural powerhouses of the town occupy virtually the entire northwestern part of town. The Old Mill Road divides us into East and West Betterton, while Main Street serves as our virtual prime meridian. In the middle of Betterton there are some well-kept homes filled with schoolteachers, policemen, the sheriff, and other stereotypical townsfolk. If we had a mayor, I'm sure he or she would live there, but we don't have one. Nobody wanted the job. In fact, the ballot has been as vacant as the expression on Deputy Upchurch's face in the middle of our Sunday go-to meeting. Eventually, the town council just absorbed all of the governing responsibilities for the locale. The state hates it, but what can they do if nobody runs for the office?

We have a railroad that cuts the town in half. It comes into town up by the Decello farm and then just sort of slices over and down like the right side of McDonald's golden arches. Right before it leaves Betterton, it cuts a line between the police and fire stations and our elementary school. Every time a train would come through, Ms. Stanton would talk louder and louder as if nothing was happening. If the whistle on the train blew, I would perk up only to see if her eyes really could pop out of her head.

In Betterton, we only have two schools, the elementary school for kindergarten to eighth grade, and Betterton Senior High. This is my senior year. I participate in the usual fare:

cheerleading, band, book club. I guess many people would tease me for not being dark and introspective enough. I have also been accused of lacking a certain bubbly personality, which could potentially be seen as flirtatious. Fact is, I'm just your normal, everyday, vanilla kind of girl. I just enjoy English, book club, FFA, and the occasional cigarette in the woods behind the school. Benton caught me there once. It was the only time I remember him looking at me without a smile. My friend Hunter McMillan had never liked the practice either.

The truth is, I like my school, my teachers, and my friends. I just don't like the halls. That is where the tension lies. The paths to and from the safe haven of classes are breeding grounds for ugly looks from members of other factions who look down their noses with self-righteous indignation. One might be strolling out of Mr. Valdez's Spanish class still practicing rolling your R's when suddenly, a resentful, loathsome expression from a passerby can puncture the comfortable atmosphere and remind you that the war rages on.

The war. When the hard times came and the mill went hollow, the light in Betterton began to dim. We lost Bradly's Shoes, Buffy's Books, a little clothing store, the bakery, and Dixie Hardware on Main. The laundry is still there, along with Spires' Grocery and the beauty shop. Doctor Mason still practices medicine and runs the pharmacy toward the end of the sidewalk. And Main Street ends at the town courthouse, where Judge Thornton Leach has been presiding for thirty-five years. He'll be at the meeting tonight too.

I find it difficult to bridge the divide between the Betterton of my childhood and the community we navigate today. The haven that once felt as if it had been drawn by the hand of God himself now feels like a combat area with safe areas, neutral zones, and dangerous enemy territory. Such a stark juxtaposition.

The root of this modern powder keg, which now permeates every aspect of daily life, can be traced back to a single man— Delbert Beechum Bethune. Most of his slowly enlarging group of minions simply call him "Beech." Extra syllables must take too much effort for people who devote so much of their time to being outraged at what they consider to be the moral wrongdoings of others.

He is an older man, late fifties to early sixties, I suppose. He is large, bearded, and bespectacled with a knob nose and a red face like a drunkard. Only Beech doesn't drink. Rumors of prior abuse linger but have never been proven.

Beech—is—a very calloused man. He got rich up north in Ohio running a large custodial service company he'd inherited from his father. Some time around the turn of the millennium, though, he abruptly closed the company and fired all of his workers after the state adopted policies favoring more diverse companies. Of Beech's one-hundred-some-odd employees, none—not one—had been black, Jewish, gay or Hispanic. It isn't hard to deduce the mindset behind such hiring practices.

After shuttering the doors of the business that had made him quite wealthy, Beech retreated for a while. Plainly put, he withdrew from society, community, and frankly, reality. I think that's when his wife left him. As Sharron tells it, one day Beech just showed up in Betterton with a wad of cash asking about buying up houses in the village. They'd been standing empty and lifeless for about a decade, and nobody else wanted them. So it took Old Man Longstreet, owner of the gas station and bowling alley and the town's only licensed realtor, quite by surprise when Beech showed such an interest in a section of town long since discarded by the natives.

Beech bought the first two houses closest to the old mill on the block of First Street and Second Avenue. He tore both places down and had a crew from Wilmington construct the two-story gothic monstrosity in which he currently resides. He then made a huge offer to the bank, which had been sitting uneasily on many of the properties that had been in foreclosure for years. Finally, he bought up the last few odd rental properties and storage shacks from their respective owners in town. Most people assumed he intended to fix up and rent the places out to turn a profit. God, I wish that had been the case.

All hopes of a return to the sparkling little area of town were shattered when *they* began to come. Random men, women, families, loners, vagrants, and other folks with no ties whatsoever to Betterton—most not even from the state of North Carolina. But they came. Beech didn't do a thing to renovate those crumbling structures unless it was required by law to keep them up to rental code. Beech lured in outsider after outsider until the town seemed full of strangers—*Eastenders*, we call them.

We weren't used to seeing unfamiliar faces in the grocery store or at the gas station. We knew everybody. Even if you were not close acquaintances, you still knew all the faces. You may even identify people by whom they associate with. Now this sudden tidal wave of unrecognizable humanity flooded us without warning. That's when the war started.

I hear Deputy's car as his headlights shine through my lace curtains. His name is Brad Vance, but I just call him Deputy. He's a little too mom's apple pie watching baseball and calling all the boys "sport" for me. But he's a good guy for a redheaded, small-town cop. Doors open and close. "Hello, Sharron." "Hey, Brad." A kiss, an invitation from Mama to come out to the car.

The ride to the town hall is queer. I can feel every bump in the road, but I can't hear any sound. I sit on my hands to keep the trembling out of visibility. A light rain taps unheard against my window pane. There is no stopping now.

As we walk into the town hall, I see *them* first. All sitting on the right of the aisle, scowling and seething. My body tenses quickly to adapt to my surroundings. I let Sharron and Deputy take their seats beside Deputy Upchurch and his wife. I take a seat near the middle by my best friend, Hunter, with whom I spend most of my Saturdays now. He is the only person, other than Sharron, with whom I feel absolutely at home no matter where we are. We met in third grade when I slapped Robby Finchwick for calling him a racial slur that does not warrant repeating. Hunter is the face I look for in the crowd at school and the last text I send each night. He isn't exactly like a boyfriend or a brother, but perhaps the best qualities of both concepts embodied in one, I must say, strikingly handsome, young man. Sharron never really tries to curtail our time together, and she certainly doesn't care about his being black. In fact, I was never aware that there was even potential for our friendship to be scrutinized or censured. I mean we had a few local idiots who parroted what they heard from their elders from a generation past, but unadulterated racism had never been so boldly manifest. Not until *they* came. Not until the war.

HUTCH

Damned traitors. Walking in and being all quiet like that won't piss off. Comin' in here mixing like mongrels. Bastardizing the races, a fag in every family. I hate the damned sight of them. Makes me sick to see these damned townie traitors persecute us and attack our religious freedoms to satisfy their liberal snowflake politically correct pussy asses. My wife thinks I'm too hardlined on some of these things. She'll say, *Hutch Inman, you gotta let other people live how they live.* Turns my damned stomach.

My family ain't from here. My wife Iris, our son Scott, and me come about a year or so ago from Georgia. Beech reached out to several of the members of my online chapter of the NSM. I knew some of the members personally, and some of them I've met since we been here. In Macon, it was hard to keep company with our own race. Seemed like everywhere we went, we run into mongrels and wetbacks. Here lately even the fags don't try and keep quiet. It's enough to make a man throw up his hands and quit. I suppose some did, but not me. I got pissed.

All this mixing and mingling just ain't how things are supposed to be. The races are just too different. We have different grooming habits, family traditions, value systems, even different diseases. I know the damned snowflakes say that last one is false, but what do you call sickle cell? All these liberal idiots try to explain away what is plain as day right in front of a man's face. They use bleeding heart "We are the world" bullshit arguments to rationalize the contamination of the white race. They run away from God because His Word and the teachings of the church strip away all that left-wing crap.

I believe in discipline. The book of Romans talks about all men being subject to laws and rules. Well, one rule is keeping to your own. It goes on to talk about consequences for men who are too weak to submit to God's laws.

Before we come here, I was just about burnt out. People were always looking down at me and saying I was racist 'cause I got a rebel flag sticker on my truck. One time a lady at the grocery store asked me, "What's your problem?" when she caught me rolling my eyes at the sight of a black wearing nicer jeans than mine and texting on his iPhone, using food stamps that I had to work hard to pay for. And she was white!

I just started to feel like our way of life was changing. Fading. Dying alone right before our very eyes. How is a man supposed to feel when everything he knows in his gut and his heart is being attacked? Pissed off. The answer is pure-t pissed off.

I done some searching on the web and found there are a whole lot more like-minded men and women across this beautiful country of *ours*. That's when I joined the National Socialist Movement. Reading their literature was like an answer to prayers. I ain't some old, outlier of a fossil clinging to a dead way of life. I'm an American man, among many, who have had it up to here with being told how to act, what to say, and who I have to mix with! I finally found people who I could talk to. People who reacted the same way to the liberalization of this country as I did. People who could see the threat to our religion and our way of life. I felt more at home online than I did in my own hometown.

That's when we found Beech. He started sending private messages and emails to NSM members talking about a *crusade to a white utopia*, free of mongrels and social deviants. A place where it was okay to be a white Christian man and not feel ashamed about it. I did some research on Beech and found out he had the cash to put his money where his faith was when he wanted to.

The day he bought the land here, he let us all know. He sent out pictures with captions telling about his ideas for what this place could become. I started dreaming of how it could be if the other members of our group would only listen and open their minds to how real this could be if we just came together and acted! But most of them thought I was crazy. They agreed in spirit, but I guess they was held back by fear. Most of them seemed to lack the fortitude to commit to action.

I emailed Beech, and it was the best move I ever made. He hadn't been only talking to our little chapter. No, he was smarter than that. He'd been reaching out to the White Knights, the Aryan Brotherhood, and other white nationalist organizations in search of true believers to join this crusade and make his dream a reality. Hell, he already had nine families by that time. My brother, who had always been a sell-out when it came to being "tolerant" of other people, tried to talk us out of leaving. But I'd had my fill. We quit renting in Macon and started renting here in Betterton from Beech.

Betterton. Just the name tells you the story. When our crusade is done, this will be the *better town* compared to any other place in the land. It will be a bright, clean example of how America could be if we hold on to the traditions that founded this country.

We moved into a small two-bedroom house on Fifth Street. I got a job pumping gas in the daytime, and I pull late shifts at the bowling alley when I can. Iris works the counter part-time at Spires' Grocery. We ain't rolling in money, but we make ends meet. Outside of work we mostly keep on our side of town, the upper east side. That's why the damned townies call us

Eastenders. We don't care. I'll wear that as a badge of pride all day long. Scott too.

When we gather amongst ourselves, we are in Heaven. We barbeque, watch football, play cards, and help Beech work on the old mill. Eventually, he wants to fix it up into apartments so more of our white brothers and sisters can join us. Beech says that all of us that help out can share in some of the rent when the day comes. It's nice having a project together, working with your own for a common goal without persecution from the blasphemous, godless idiots that infect our modern American society.

It's when we have to mix with the townies that things can get a little dicey. We call them that because on more than one occasion, we have heard several of them say stupid shit like "This is our town" or "You can't do that in our town." They cling on to this place like it's still what it was fifteen years ago. Well, we got news for them. It ain't! I mean we tried to attend church and all with them, but that preacher rambled on about acceptance and tolerance and attacking us for having pride in our race. We just couldn't take that no more. Now we have our own man of God. The Reverend Hartley Ray came here about eight months back. We been holding our own service in some of the improved rooms at the mill. Beech says we will build a church of our own soon after we finish up with the mill. That's what these townies don't understand. We ain't here to destroy. We are here to build!

The way they ran the place damned near ended it for good. Betterton was on a dying path when Beech came here to save it. But the townies don't feel that way. They act like they've been invaded! Set upon by people they'd rather look down on and judge rather than listen to and learn. Ya can't hardly blame people for pushing back when they feel talked down to and scorned. Hell, that's how they're all looking at me now sitting in this damned town hall, looking out the corners of their eyes and whispering God knows what to each other. Why can't they open their eyes and see? Our side is as it should be! That side, all jumbled up with whites and blacks and browns and God knows what all is an abomination! Just look at that retard over there playing with that phone. I know he don't understand what he's doing and my tax dollars probably paid for it. Damned shame. He's over there smiling like an idiot while we are forced to wait on the morons on the town council to figure out what to do about the "conflict" and "unrest" that has befallen their poor little Betterton.

I guess it couldn't be helped, being that this place ain't exactly immense, that eventually tension would lead to confrontation. I heard about a few little dustups at the high school, but you know, boys will be boys. I told Scott that he would not face no consequences from me for standing up for his principles at home or school. Then some of the townie parents started bitching at Principal Lewis about the kids having rebel flags on their cars and their clothes. Can you believe that? Calling a schoolhouse trying to attack people's First Amendment right to free speech?

I know a few of us have had some words with the townies. Nothing major, just standing up for our beliefs. It did get a little heated at the bowling alley a couple of times, but hell, it couldn't be helped. The final straw from the townies come when some property got damaged. Seems one of our kids pulled a prank and spray-painted a swastika on Bill Decello's barn door. I know it ain't right to mess with another man's land, but he should be man enough to explain to his son that white boys are supposed to date white girls. That boy had been holding hands and kissing on that Valdez girl for months and he had not done a damned thing about it.

Rest assured I told Scott what was what. It'll be the same with my nephew, Trent, when he gets here next week. My brother died last month and his wife Anne, weak as ever, got herself addicted to a stiff mix of painkillers and booze. She's been checked into some facility to dry out, so Trent will come and stay with us. He ain't the most principled, disciplined young man you ever met. Can't hardly blame him with a father gone and a mother in Anne's state. Living with us will do him good.

Damn it! Special privileges for mongrels and sexual deviants? We can't let this stand. Beech won't let this stand. He's filed to run for sheriff against Teal. With our numbers, I like his chances.

My buddy Mack Ivey starts to crack a joke but the gavel bangs. Council is coming in. Lord help me hold my tongue. Let these bastards come down on the right side.

"Order! Order here! This council has deliberated in executive session for the third and final time in consideration of the town ordinance banning and penalizing discrimination of any citizen based on their race, religion, sexual orientation, or identity. The measure calls for all citizens to be protected, and it provides that violation of the measure could result in a fine of $1,000 and/or 30 days in the city jail. By a final tally of 5-2 the measure passed and the ordinance will go into effect tonight."

"Disgraceful, the lot of them. Damned disgraceful!"

TRENT

These eggs taste like crap, but at least Aunt Iris tries. My mom only turned the stove on to light a smoke, so I guess this is better. I mean, hey, don't thump a free melon, right?

Scott's car smells like weed, but who am I to judge? As we park by the school, I can't help but think this must be the smallest high school in the country. One parking lot, one building. On the way in I spot the sports "complex," a football field and a baseball diamond that I assume the softball team shares, if they even have a softball team. Across the street from the school, they got a joint called the Finer Diner and a shady bowling place. That's it. All of it. Ten seconds to take it all in.

I spend the first hour of the day waiting on my schedule, playing pool on my phone, getting snaps from girls I knew in Georgia, and trying not to notice the fact that every time I look up, the secretary is looking right at me. I'm eighteen, I know that look, and you're out of luck. Still, it makes me smile a little. I never really mind being noticed.

A crow-looking lady in a legit pantsuit finally calls me up to the counter.

"Mr. Inman, I have your schedule. Unfortunately, we do not offer all of the courses that you were taking at your old school, but I tried my best to make do. I'll walk you to your first class."

Mrs. Lewis's shoes clack real loud as we head down the hall to Ms. Oberry's English IV class. She seemed nice enough and not bad to look at, even at her age.

"Where should I sit? Just anywhere?" I was eyeballing a seat next to this cute redhead chewing on her pencil and pretending not to notice me. I love when girls do that.

"Nah, man. You're here," says a random guy I've never seen before, but I felt kinda boxed in at that point. So, cop a squat.

"I'm Clinton Kitchens. This is Melvin Jackson. Them over there's the Dillingham brothers. Two of 'em are twins. One's just a dumbass in the same grade as his kid brothers."

"I'm Trent, man. Nice to meet ya," I whispered as Ms. Oberry was clearly ready to restart class. She started talking all excited like about whatever book I'm sure I'll get a copy of tomorrow that they all have today. I tried to pay attention for a solid five minutes, but I knew I'd have to hang back after class to figure out what they've been doing and at least half ass make an effort to catch up.

As much as I try to look like I'm legit intrigued by what she's talking about, I keep chancing a glance over there at Red. Her hair is so full and long. She's got it tucked behind one ear. I love when girls do that. They want you to see their faces, you know. And I do see. Her eyes are like crystals, I swear. Lips full and plump. Her dress is on point, and she's giving it a run for its money. Why am I not sitting by Red again?

The phrases "kick his ass" and "break his face" bring me right out of my little romantic fog just in time for the bell. I wanted to make my way over to say hi or something, but these dudes, Clinton and Melvin, sort of pushed me out the door.

Clinton advises me, "Be careful, Trent. We stick with our own here, even in school. We know you're Scott's cousin. Try and meet the others from the east end. They'll take care of you."

Melvin looks at the schedule in my hand. "You'll want Norton, Science lab. Two doors down on the left."

"Thanks, man," I said, taking a sip of water and a moment to notice the natives all noticing me. I'm not what you might call assertive, but I like to get noticed.

Science is a little less crowded than English. I go up to the front and show my schedule to Mr. Norton, who no joke looks just like Bill Nye, the Science guy. When I turn to find my spot to kill time for the rest of the semester, my faith in God is restored. Red's in this class too.

"Hey, I'm Trent. Anyone sit in this one?" She smells like soap and peaches.

"No, all yours," she says without looking up. This ignoring me crap won't do. I say, "So, you got a name or should I just call you Red?"

Now I got her attention, only not the way I want. Those beautiful, crystal blue eyes become like knives being hurled my way.

"I. Hate. That. Name."

"Whoa, I'm really sorry. I didn't mean to offend you. I'm new here. Ain't quite settled in yet."

That seems to disarm her some. I throw in my best little smile for good measure.

"Sorry, long day. I'm Addison," she says, reaching out to shake my hand. "Addison it is."

I sit through the rest of science class mesmerized by her perfume and the way she uncrosses and re-crosses her legs every five minutes like clockwork. Twenty minutes in, some random black dude rolls in late with a yellow slip in his hand.

"Sorry, Mr. Norton, dentist."

"No problem, Hunter. Take your seat."

That seat happens to be on the opposite side of Red, I mean Addison. I won't say he was looking at me shady or dirty, but he doesn't seem thrilled to see me sitting there either. No time for introductions now.

At the end of class, I write my digits on a torn-off piece of paper and pass them to Addison while she packs her things to leave. She seems like a modern, assertive, women's-rights kind of girl, but she's still a girl. She'll know what to do. I did try to speak to random dentist dude before he left.

"Hey man, I'm Trent." All I got back was "All right."

At lunch, Scott walks me over to the table where I assume he normally eats. I recognize the Dillinghams. Turns out there's four. Shaw and Will are twins. They're seniors. George, the older brother who is on the reunion tour of senior year, goes by Biscuit. The youngest, whom Biscuit said they all call "the accident," is Neil. They all look like they come from a family tree that don't branch.

I also meet Brett Ivey and Sarah Ellison. There's nothing dumb looking about either of these two. They seem smart and serious as a case of crabs.

We eat and make small talk for the next fifteen minutes or so. I ask if they had a good baseball team, but they said they were awful. I'll find something better to do in my spare time. I'm headed to throw away the little crusty bits of lunch that are left on my styrofoam tray when I hear this sudden spike in sound. When I turn around, someone slides toward me on his back with blood coming out of his nose.

As I'm trying to both figure this the hell out and step out of the way, I see Clinton and Melvin both reach down and pick up the bloody sliding dude and push him through the cafeteria doors into the hallway. A circle promptly forms while they beat the crap out of this kid, two on one, and nobody does anything to stop it. By now at my old school, a couple of big football players would have tried to help or a teacher would have made it or something. This poor kid just takes almost a minute-long beating before, finally, the school resource officer breaks through and threatens to pepper spray all three of them. That's about all he could do, I imagine. He looks like he's a hundred.

I catch the looks on the faces of my pals from lunch. They don't look scared or shocked at all. They just looked . . . I dunno, satisfied I think. It's weird.

After lunch I gotta do PE with Coach Mercer. He seems cool enough, and I can think of worse ways to pass ninety minutes than playing basketball. There's only like ten of us here anyway. What else would we do?

Shit. Hunter's in this class. And, bonus, he gets picked to be a captain. My lucky day: Coach makes me the other captain because I'm the new kid.

Hunter's first three picks are the two other black kids and the one Hispanic dude. My team ends up all white 'cause that's all that was left.

After teams are picked, I join Hunter in the center circle. I stick my hand out and say, "Good luck, man." Again, all I get is, "All right." What's this dude's deal?

For the next hour we play what I can only describe as the sloppiest, most violent basketball game I have ever been a part of. We all caught, and threw, more elbows, jabs, picks, and other fouls than should ever be allowed on a court, much less in a high school gym. But Coach seems to have a "rubbin's racin'" sort of attitude. Either that or he is allergic to that whistle.

After the game, we head back to the locker room to change. I grab a towel from the stack and head back to at least rinse this sweat off before my last class. I walk toward the echo of the water and go to take a left where I see open showerheads. An arm grabs me. I sort of jerk my arm away as I turn around a bit surprised. It's one of the kids on my basketball team.

"We don't use those. We use these," he says, nodding to the showers on the other side of the little hallway that divided the area in half. I just go with it.

As the warm water washes away any traces of that awful game, apart from the bruises I know I'm going to see tomorrow, it dawns on me what Clinton must have meant by "stick with your own." They must take that crap really seriously here.

After I dry off and get my clothes back on, I see the light on my phone. I missed a text from a number I didn't know. It reads, "So you had an eventful first day. Wild lunch. Just wanted to make sure you came through okay."

I text back, "Yeah, I'm good. Who is this?" and set out to find my math class, which I know I have with Scott. I think it's good to end the day with him since he's my ride.

I feel my phone vibrate, so I swipe and check the text. The random number sends back a single word.

"Addison."

SHARRON

I am unable to envision what a Sunday would be without my ascension of these stone stairs, the interlacing of fingers with my only child, and the reassuring salutation Benton exudes every time we appear. I gingerly trace the smooth grooves of the railing with one finger in my approach more out of formality than utility. This church is sustenance for me. Sometimes it finds me strong, in command, ready to pray to Him for paths to forge in life and love and longing. Lately, I come here shaky, unsure, sometimes bruised and broken.

This carpet needs replacing. Still, it muffles the clatter of my heels as we make our way to the pew, which hosts us each Sunday. Brad's smile is a warm greeting as I tuck my skirt under my legs and examine the program to see which hymns I should bookmark this morning.

It is rather peculiar, the things that distract you when you allow your mind to be still. These last weeks have been so confoundingly insecure. I confess myself unaccustomed to indecision or lacking in confidence, but recently the predictable has proven elusive, replaced by the undetermined, the unsettled, the unreasonable. At least in this haven, I can allow my subconscious to roam. My eyes follow a single speck of dust as the ornate stained glass windows illuminate its descent into the aisle that brought me here.

The sudden sound of the organ and the shifting noises of my cohorts positioning themselves upright and ready to worship shocks me into the present. Addison and Brad proceed me in standing from the pew to sing a song of cheerful welcome. It is reflexive, this verse. It envelops the whole of the congregation in a blanket of fellowship and ease of spirit. I find myself singing it without concern for meaning. I do not send my words aloft like a prayer—rather, I follow suit with the preordained routine. This allows my eyes and mind time to meander.

My familiarity with the majority of the flock seems surprisingly restored. It would appear that the temporary imposition on the part of the occupants of the village has reached its conclusion. At least the perpetual potential for petty engagement no longer pervades the pews. I gather that our message of unity, hope, and tolerance was unpalatable for the Eastenders, so they have established a new place to congregate on the Sabbath.

A final note reverberates over the parishioners as the organ returns to silence at the direction of its operator. A shuffling sound covers the coughs and throat clearings as we guide ourselves back to our stations.

Sally Grist has played the organ here for as long as memory serves. Her brother, Billy, sings in the choir alongside Big Jack Simmons, Marshall Crawford, William Lynch, Brady Price, dear Decon Decello, and a few other rotating members of the gentlemen's division. The ladies' brigade invariably consists of the honorable, yet not intolerable, Mrs. Sarah Cooper, Ella Dunbar, Nancy Lewis, and Chelsea McClain, the last of whom is rumored to get around this municipality like a ceiling fan, if you will be kind enough to excuse the vulgarity of the thought.

As Reverend Pruitt articulates what is no doubt a loquacious rendition of his recently redundant call for us to proceed steadfastly unified in defiance of the forces that would otherwise threaten the cohesive fabric of Betterton, my thoughts go astray. I notice Addison, and I think of what truly vexes me. It is not my fellow church members that heighten my anxiety.

It is the growing swell of ever stranger settlers here in Betterton that give me pause. Brad told me six new families moved in over the last month. My daughter refers to the situation as a *war*. How bleak that seems.

More than their presence, it is the vulgarity of their views and means of expressing them that make me worry for my daughter. From the dawn of her life she has been reared to be independent and strong, but with a gentle heart and welcoming disposition. I wonder if I have armed her with defenses sufficient to combat what is undoubtedly a growing chasm between Addison and her cohorts and the Eastenders at school. The physical assault on Little Jack Simmons this week stands as another caution to me.

Benton breaks my concentration with the offering plate. It's uncanny how in a single glance one can leave the foreboding, ominous path of trepidation and grim expectation and be transported to such a thoroughfare of comfort and reassurance. The innocence and love that Benton exudes with his earnest smile and gentle, compassionate eyes remind me of how much goodness and light are still here. Perhaps he is the reason I came today. Perhaps Benton is a sign from God that hope may be waxing rather than waning.

A reflexive smile dances across my face as I turn to see Addison doubtlessly having similar thoughts. Brad seems oblivious, but then why deviate from the norm? I am glad he is in my life, though he has not yet successfully penetrated the barriers of the fortress I constructed around my heart when Addison's father absconded after learning that she was on the way. Still, Brad is here in the present. In time I may grow to love him. For the present I enjoy the company. My thoughts begin to turn to matters that are altogether inappropriate to contemplate in church. I steel my mind as the crescendo of Reverend Pruitt's voice signals the end of his sermon.

It is time to sing again.

LITTLE JACK

I 've always hated the name "Little Jack." They only call me that because my mom thought Jack Jr. sounded too white. It never bothered my dad, but then again Dad is white so I guess it wouldn't. I suppose it was cute when I was a little boy, but now it makes me feel trapped in childhood. It also makes me sound silly and unintelligent. I am neither of those.

I guess I also have an aversion to it because nicknames make people stand out. Like nobody remembers which Bill or Ted or Tyrone you saw in the hall yesterday but Tall Tommie or Ragin' Ray, those guys had to be noticed. I don't need any more reasons to get noticed. I'm six feet two inches tall, one of like four biracial students at school, and I am number one in the junior class. I would stand out even more if anyone other than one baseball player and a friend from up the street knew I have no interest in girls whatsoever. What. So. Ever.

I suppose you might find it surprising to learn that the highlight of my week is actually church. Well, not the Sunday school part, but the service is usually awesome. I love to sing; I love a good story and I'm always up for a speech about unity and nonjudgment. Bonus, I get to wear my best clothes. I like to be well put together, but I have to save my best for Sundays. Double bonus, we get to eat at the Finer Diner after church. It's not the food that I like as much as it is the guy that brings it to the table. He graduated a few years ago, but not from Betterton. Mexican dude. I'd never say anything to him other than my order and a polite thank-you. Still, looking is free. Though, I'm pretty sure he never looks back.

If he did today, he'd be asking about my swollen eye and lip. I was not surprised to be confronted; it just caught me off guard that there were two of them. At least give a guy a shot.

The quirky thing about it, at least to me, is that they didn't do it because I'm half black, and I know they didn't do it because I'd be more into them than I would be their sisters. They challenged me because I embarrassed Melvin Jackson in Mrs. Reid's U.S. history class. He tried making arguments that the United States is a Christian country founded on Christian values and in which English is the national language. A quick Google search on my phone gave me, "The government of the United States is not, in any sense, founded on the Christian religion." - John Adams. On that junk about English being the official language, I suppose it was a little overkill to laugh out loud, literally, when Mrs. Reid pointed out that the U.S. has no official language.

I could see his little blond eyebrows clench and his face flush red. An hour later, I'm the one embarrassed getting my ass kicked by two albino assholes. At least I know I won't run into Clinton or his little friend Melvin—who the hell names a kid Melvin since 1985? —for at least the first three days of this week. Bye, Felicia.

The whole event flashed one last time when I saw the school across the street as we walked from the car to the door of the diner. Then, there he was. Hot as ever.

The first time I saw him, I remember thinking, "Pleeease be my waiter, Pablo or Angel or whatever your name is." Turned out it was Josh and I felt like an asshole.

Today we will be taken care of by Shelly. She's perfectly nice, but she's no Josh. As a consolation prize, I let myself risk a glare at the new kid, Trent. Only for a moment; he didn't see me. I know he's one of *them*. Still, cute is cute.

The food came as Mom and Dad were having a thrilling discussion about changing health insurance agencies or whatever adults talk about when their kids are spaced out and in their own worlds. I only noticed them because they stopped talking and Dad cleared his throat. He was focused on something behind and above me, so I turned around and locked eyes with Clinton, Melvin, and what I assumed were their fathers. The one that was with Melvin approached my dad, seated beside my mother across from me.

"Look," he said, his face all smug and full of himself, "I know kids get into things at school. But I don't think it's near fair that my son got three days out and your boy," my dad bristled at the word *boy*, "gets off scot-free."

"Well, according to Principal Lewis, the camera showed these two boys were the aggressors. My son was attacked from behind," he said, gesturing toward Clinton and his pal, the constitutional scholar.

Then Kitchens piped up. "Well, your Little Jack here did try to make fun and laugh at my son in class. You don't think that's bullying?"

"I am not sure what did or did not happen in class. I was not there. But my *son* did not instigate a violent altercation." Dad seemed irritated at the insinuation that I was at fault. Like I, the ass kickee, was actually the bully. He went on, "It was your sons who used fists as intimidation, not mine."

"Intimidation?" Mr. Jackson asked, angrily and loudly drawing the attention of everyone in the place. He seemed to notice that fact instantly. He looked around like he was searching for something to do now that he had an audience.

"Yes. Intimidation. Was that a question of your not agreeing with the premise or did you want a definition of the term?" Ah. So I get it from Dad. A few snickers from somebody in the back sent Kitchens over the edge.

"You ain't seen intimidation!" he yelled, balling up his fist. Before I could move, Jackson had his meathooks holding me in the booth. Dad could hardly stand with Mr. Kitchens bearing down on him and his legs stuck in the booth.

I heard Mama scream something. Then I felt a weight holding me down, and I had to watch helplessly as Craig Kitchens grabbed Dad's tie with his left hand and bashed him in the face twice with his right. Dad lurched right to try and break Kitchens' grip, knocking Mom's milkshake all over her dress and sort of pinning her in the corner of the booth.

Well, Kitchens let him go. He knew he'd lost his cool in front of too many witnesses. The four of them lit out the door, jumped into a pickup truck with a rebel flag bumper sticker, and sped off.

For a second the place froze. All I heard was one dish somewhere clanging to a stop. My eyes darted around just long enough to see everyone else in the diner doing the same. Then my eyes fell on Mom. Her eyes were filled with shock and tears, and her favorite yellow church dress was covered in chocolate. She put both hands on Dad's face to examine the damage.

Something happens to you when you see tears from your mother. Don't get me wrong; my heart broke for my father too, but something about Mama's tears tore me open.

Suddenly several people we know from church stood up and tried to help. Mrs. Grist, the lady who does music, tried to help Mama clean her dress, and Mr. Crawford came to check on Dad. Shelly appeared with a napkin full of ice.

And me. Frozen. Worthless. All of this was my fault for getting my jollies in class. Now I've been jumped, Dad got punched in the face, and Mama was humiliated.

I'm not sure which of the next parts of the day were worse—waiting for Officer Upchurch to arrive on the scene or explaining to him that I sat there like a bitch.

One thing was very clear though, and every person in the room felt it as strongly as I did—between the townies and the Eastenders, something broke that day. In an instant, irreversible way. All the tension had finally caught fire, and there was no way of knowing who would get burned next.

HUNTER

"**B**ruh, what the shit was that?" my teammate Alex asks me like I know what the hell was going on. I'm sitting here eating my fries and minding my damn business. I saw those white dudes come in, but I ain't pay attention to what they was saying. I had my earbuds in trying to drown in some Kendrick Lamar. I ain't know anything was going on 'til I saw dude punch Lil Jack's dad in the face. I pulled my buds out, but they was out the door before I could get right in my head what was happening.

I mean, me and Jack ain't really friends, but them Eastend dudes are messed up for coming for dude's family. I kinda stay back from him myself. I don't want him getting nothing confused. Him and me had a little, well, experiment behind the bathrooms at the tennis courts freshman year, but I'm not really into all that. But I did walk over and ask if he was all right. He ain't even look up at me. Just sat there looking all hard and mad.

I put my tunes back and throw my shades on as we came out the diner. I can't be out in public not looking tight. You can be jealous of my polo and my fade. I like that. Admire me, but do it at a distance.

It's nice to be able to ride through town in a fly car. It's used, but still on point. My dad works at a dealership in Cumberland. Mom used to teach English, but she don't work now.

I texted Addison on the way back to the house to see if she wanted to go for a run later. Cheerleaders and basketball players need to keep up, you know. She ain't text me back 'til I was back home. I told her I'd change my clothes and meet her at the school parking lot. We could run around the track by the football field. It's hot as shit, but I haven't run since last week.

I pulled into the parking lot and spotted Addison talking to Benton. Sometimes he hangs around the school when it's closed. He picks up trash and pecans, takes pics of the fields, and talks to anyone who happens by. He's harmless.

"Hey, Benton!" He grinned at me and showed me a pic of his cat. I think it's a cat. Might be a rabbit. Who knows? It was so out of focus.

"Yeah, man. That's cool." Benton headed back toward the front of the school.

"Thought you was going to ignore me. How was church?" I asked. We didn't go today. I was up late doing . . . well, I was up late.

Addison says, "You know I don't ignore you. Sharron was a little *extra* today after church. She doesn't talk about it much, but I know she's worried that the town is headed for an all-out war. I didn't see the text until after lunch."

"Since you mentioned it, I thought you might have been with your Eastend boy, what's his name?"

"Trent? He's not my boy. I mean we do text a little here and there. He flirts some, but I get the feeling he does that with every female he comes into contact with. I guess he's nice enough. He doesn't seem as . . . I don't know, hard core as the rest of them. I don't know, I only met him last week."

"I don't like any of them. Damned dixie flags and sideways looks. And that Nazi shit on the barn was messed up. I don't know if this new tolerance ordinance or whatever is going to help or make them worse." I told her about what I saw in the diner. I left out the part about me and Lil Jack and the tennis courts.

"I still can't believe Bethune is actually running against Sheriff Teal. Seems like they're taking over the whole town. Sharron and Deputy put a Teal sign in our yard, but someone snatched it out of the ground."

We don't talk when we run. Addie doesn't go as fast as me, but it's cool having someone to be out here with. I don't really feel threatened in town, but I do get the feeling like it would be too easy to drift too far away from friendlies and catch a case of being black around too many Eastenders. Besides, when I run, I like to let go. I don't have to worry about anything. I can think clearly, and I don't have to answer to anybody. It's like I'm flying. She likes music when she works out, but I like the sound of the air and the feel of my blood pumping.

This Trent dude just seems shady to me. You can't hang around racist ass people like that and be okay with it unless you feel some kind of way yourself. If you ain't with it, step from it. But if you're in it, you gotta own it. That's all I'm saying.

Plus he's cocky, like he thinks he's fine and every girl is picking up what he's throwing down. I hate to tell him, he ain't never going to beat a black man in that department, for real.

I like Addie, so I do have her back. I don't want her getting messed up with the wrong dude and then I have to step in and get my ass in trouble.

I have to put it out of my mind and focus on the track. The whole damned team should be out here running with me. That's our biggest problem. They get out of breath halfway through the second half of games. They can hang, but they're lazy and won't listen to Coach. I break a sweat at least three times a week. This season I want us to do better, but everybody has to want it as bad as me.

When we finish chugging water after we run, we always stretch before we head out. Addison don't drive so I'll take her home even though she walked here from her house.

"Given any thought to what college you want to look at after next year? Sharron wants me to look at NC State, but I was thinking about trying for NYU. Shoot for the stars, right?"

"Nah, I got another year. Coach says he's going to send some film to some small colleges and see. I don't have straight A's but my grades are still pretty good I guess."

"Yeah, 'cause you study with me!" she said smiling. I like the way she smiles, but I look away to try to hide it when I see two dudes hopping into a truck in the parking lot. I couldn't see their faces, but they were in an awful hurry to get out of here.

"Who was that?" she asked.

"I couldn't see. Come on." Heading back to the car, I pressed a little more about Trent.

"You would say something back to him if he said anything against us, wouldn't you? I mean, you wouldn't just be quiet?"

"Who is us?" she asked. She had to know what I meant, but I answered her question. "Black people. Or people like you that hang around with black people. Or people that don't hate black people. You know, regular people. Not people like them."

"We've barely met, but yes. Of course I would say something. Haven't you met me?" She smiled again as we topped the hill headed back to the parking lot. That's when I saw it.

"What the fuck?" I don't usually talk like that around girls, but it was out of my mouth before I knew it. "What is this shit?"

"Oh my God. Oh God," was all she said. Her voice broke and stole my attention away from my car. She was scared. I couldn't be mad then. I had to get her home safe first.

"I'm all right. You're all right. Let's get you home. I'll call the police from your house if you think your mom won't care." She ain't say anything. Just got into the car crying.

I drove her home through town in my 2015 Maxima, which now had the word *coon* spray-painted on the damn hood.

7

HUTCH

Every time I cross these railroad tracks on Old Mill Road headed south, my stomach turns a bit. Gotta leave the good, clean streets of the village and cross through this pack of mix-matched mutts and mongrels. And my feeling on it is, if you white and you associate and fraternize with them, you might as well be one. You lay down with trash and you wake up smelling like it. That's all I'm saying.

This old crew cab ain't much, but she's mine. Today she's dragging me through the asshole of the town down to the sheriff's station on the edge of town below the elementary school—another abomination of mixing and mingling.

I ain't saying what Craig and Eddie done to that Simmons man was right, but I get why they done it. Them townies love to embarrass those of us that believe in white Christian values. They think they're so smart with their tolerance and their learning. You put any of those bastards in the woods for five minutes and they'd be dead before they could think about what they'd find to eat. Snowflakes.

I turn left off Old Mill, pass the elementary school abomination, and follow on down to the station.

Kitchens and Jackson don't look too bad for a couple of boys who've been in the clink for two weeks.

"'Sup, boys?" I'm glad to see them both. Hell, it took forever for the judge to set them free with a court date.

"You're a sore for sighted eyes, ain'tcha! Met a fellow in there I'd bet my house you'd take a liking too. Wanna knock over Spires' Grocery so's y'all can meet up?" Eddie Jackson loves to pull my chain!

"Just get in, smartass. At least they let y'all go in time for the Fall Festival. Can't believe this'll be my second year not doing Oktoberfest in Georgia. I miss them days, but we'll make do with you, ugly jack rabbits."

Leaving the station heading for the park, I come up to the water tower and hang a right onto Old Mill Road. Sometimes I'd like to shoot a hole in the bottom of that old thing so it could wash the town clean of the filth that infects it, but luck ain't found me yet. Come back across the tracks, thank God, and park down by Fourth Avenue on the edge of the village. Betterton Park is right between our section of town and the ass end of town hall. It's almost like a buoy between the boat and the dock. Ain't much to it, but it's usually clean. Today it's filled with a mix of our folks and theirs. Don't quite sit right on my mind.

Them burgers and dogs do smell good, but I ain't having none. Craig, Eddie, Mack, and some others may not mind eating in the Finer Diner with God knows what all, but I prefer food fixed at the house by my wife to where I know who's had their hands on it since it comes out the packaging.

At least the music is all right even if it ain't live. I used to like to play some after the barbecue competition when we lived in Georgia. Can't sing for shit, but it was a good time all the same. I do love the sound of twin fiddles.

But we ain't here to eat and dance. We're here to cheer on Beech and a couple other fellows giving their speeches. The election is next month, and all the political types are using this as a time to try and be seen and heard.

When they pull the plug on the tunes, we all sort of shuffle to the middle, us on the right and them on the left. They got a little makeshift stage-like setup with room in the front for folks to gather. The candidates are all on the stage, most of them unopposed except the sheriff. Look like a bunch of idiots to me, but Lord, you can tell they think they're special. Up there with their American flag pins and crosses on their coats. Most of them don't know a damned thing about loving God or country 'til it's time to get folks to vote again.

Hadn't really thought about it until I can see it plain as day, but our bunch is a might bigger than it used to be. Had three new families join us last week from Nebraska of all places. Hope the hell they got registered to vote. Deadline was this morning.

There's five seats on the council, and it's based off areas of town. It should be just by popular vote, but the damned council keeps it like it is so the townies keep control. It's the way they kept in charge, back when the Muldune Mill was still running is what Beech says. Two members of the council get elected from the village. The rest is townies.

The three returning townies are first up to speak. The Valdez guy that teaches at the schoolhouse is first. Standing up there in his damned suit like he is a regular man's man. He ought to go back where he came from and fix things there before running for office here, but nobody asked my damned opinion.

Rusty Odom who runs the diner come after him. He yacked about taxes and small business giving back to schools. Just sounded real braggy to me. Then he sat back down in his chair on the stage next to the beaner like they are equals. And of course, not one word about God or country. Just pisses me off.

Like that little girl up yonder on the townie side talking to the darkie. All right, now she's a perfect example. Pretty little redhead like that ought to be talking to a white young man who can do right by her in life. Have kids, support her. Lead a good, God-fearing Christian life but no. She disrespects her heritage and shames her family talking to the likes of him.

Townies clap nice like when their candidates are through. Our side claps with more feeling than theirs when Alvin Dillingham gets up to talk. First thing he does is thank God for being there. See? A man's man.

He's in the middle of his patriotic tribute to American values when I see my own nephew walk up and strike up a conversation with that mixed couple of townies. I ain't going to yell at him. Hell, that would draw too much attention to it. Damn sure don't want everybody else to see my family taking part in such an ugly sight. I guess at least he's mostly talking to her, not the other kid. Hell, maybe he's trying to bring her to her senses. Still sets my teeth on edge. Walk away, Trent, just walk away. You don't want that tail if it's been all around the jungle.

Scott made his way over to me through the crowd. He seen it too. Just nodded my attention over that way.

"I know, I saw it. Don't say nothing here and for God's sake don't go over there with them."

"I know, Daddy. I just don't know how to get through to him. I mean, he don't argue with me or nothing. He just sort of shirks me off."

"How you mean?" I want to hear this.

"You know. He just listens and shrugs his shoulders. Sometimes he'll half ass agree with me like 'I guess' or 'I suppose,' but he just don't seem to take it quite to heart that we are different from them and we don't mix."

I love my brother to this day, and I miss him something awful. But his value system wasn't as principled as mine. That's why his wife was let to get on all them pills and shit. No discipline. He never could take her in hand. Iris will have a beer every now and again, but she's a lady and proper wife and mama. Trent's daddy used to say my beliefs and rules and everything were "extreme" and that I should "lighten up." My view is, why have principles and values at all if you don't live your life by them all the time? This wishy-washy shit about political correctness and only following a righteous path when it's convenient is what leads to racial impurity, sexual immorality, drugs, and immigrants, and queers, and the downfall of America!

No, sir. Not in my house.

Trent seen me and headed back to the correct side.

"Boy, what are you doing over there? Who the hell are they?"

"Her? That's Addison from school and her friend Hunter. He's on the basketball team." "And *he's* dating *her*?" Hell, he looks confused at my question.

"No, sir, they're just friends." Excuses. "We'll talk at home, son. Teal's up next."

Teal. Sorry excuse for a man. He'll probably win again, but he ain't got my vote. God, I hope Beech beats his ass. He talked in front of us at church last Sunday in the mill and really sounded good. He's a very persuasive man. He can make just about any reasonable person see his side of things.

The paper, which come from Fayetteville not here, says Teal is "an upright citizen and lifelong resident of Betterton who always does his civic duty with consistency and good ethics." Even in sleepy North Carolina, the media gets behind the most liberal jackass they can find. You can't trust half of what any of those bastards write.

Teal's just like that preacher them townies got talking about bringing the town together and unity and all that shit. How can you have unity with a bunch of blacks and browns that come from God knows where? I caught a glimpse of the town simpleton playing on his damned phone, taking pictures of all the candidates. I just shook my head.

More polite clapping when he finishes his bull.

Our side roared to life when Beech got up. He won't say the exact same thing here as he did for us Sunday. Hell, he told us he wouldn't. Said he'd "tone it down to be more sheriff-like." But we know what's in his heart.

"My fellow citizens of Betterton, we appreciate the years of service that Mr. Teal has given the town. We don't take from him his record of low crime and safe schools.

"But the fact is he does not do enough to seek out, arrest, and prosecute illegal immigrants on the farms on the west side, and we all know they're there. Their kids are soaking up tax dollars at the elementary schools that *you* pay for your own children. He does not investigate abuses of power by the town council. He simply allows them to run the town and spend all your money without any oversight whatsoever. And he sure as heck does not do a thing about some citizens who we know are taking advantage of food stamps and free meals. That's not to mention the fact that there are no new programs in this town to attract or support new businesses.

"It's time for a change here in Betterton. If we act now, we can save this town. I will fight for your freedoms, your religious liberties, and *our* shared American, Christian values. God bless Betterton, and God bless America. Thank you."

Now *that* is an American patriot right there! And our side sure does agree with him! He gets a healthy cheer from this side and a couple of nodding heads and polite claps from the townies.

I figured that was that after Beech spoke. I set my mind to what I'd say to Trent when we get to the truck. I sure as hell wasn't staying longer than needed.

But before the crowd could break up good, Deputy Vance, there's another one, stood up at the microphone and said he had an announcement.

"Folks, it looks like we have one more person to hear from." He didn't sound happy. My ears perked up.

"It seems, for the first time in quite a while, we do have one candidate actually running for mayor. Mr. Little, would you like to say a few words?"

Who the hell is Mr. Little? I looked left to see which one of them was going to take the stage, but I got caught by surprise when someone pushed their way by me on my right.

"Hey, I know that guy!" I said to Scott. "Beech helped him and his family settle in last month. I didn't know his last name. Beech called him Skinny or something."

"He filed to run today at 11:58. Deadline was noon. He's running unopposed. Too late to field an opponent it seems." There stood Phil Allistor, the closest thing we have to a deacon in our church, smiling like he'd known the whole time.

"Beech got one of ours to run for mayor?" I asked. Stunned. Why hadn't we thought of that before?

"Yes, sir. Kept it as quiet as possible 'til the last minute. You should have seen them at the courthouse when he came in with his papers and filing fee. Their jaws damn near fell off. Dewayne Little is his name, but you're right, folks do call him Twig. I think he's from Iowa. Good guy, I understand. Appreciates our values, if you know what I mean."

"Well, I'll be damned!" I looked at Scott, who seemed like he was as shocked as me. "Even if we lose the sheriff race, at least we'll have some check on the council and their stupid tolerance ordinance BS! Beech is a genius!"

I patted my boy on the back, one proud papa. It was something to see the faces of them townies when they were gathering up their shit to get out of there. They looked shocked. If they'd had half a brain, they'd have run one of their own, but Beech caught them sleeping! Now we'll see some changes in this town! On with the crusade!

ADDISON AND TRENT

Still feels like we are at war with the people in the village, and he wants to know what I'm up to...*was about to study for Monday's Spanish test. Just helped Sharron with dishes lol. U?*

Why does this girl get to me like this every time we text? *Not studying Spanish lol. Avoiding my cuz. He's annoying AF.*

Classy. *Is there something I can do for u?*

You don't know the half of it. *Just wanted to see if ya wanted to meet up or something...*

Meet up? Does he mean hook up? Hell no. And what is "or something." *Could u b more vague? LOL*

Probably. What is there to do in this burg? *Could walk in the park...* dude that's stupid...*or go bowling or something.*

Bowling? *Last time I went to the alley I caught some old man checking out my butt.*

Can't say I blame him. *You got any ideas?*

Hmm...*I could always eat. Buy me a burger? Finer Diner?*

YES! I mean, *Sure that's fine. Perfect actually, Scott and Uncle H don't go there.*

So? *Scared?*

Yeah. *More like not in the mood. Meet you in 20?*

Hmm...*Gimme 30.*

Perfect. *TTYL, see ya soon ;)*

I don't know why I'm nervous. We talk every day at school and we text like every night. I mean, not about serious shit, but we like check in. I can't figure if she's like, teasing me? Or if she's really keeping me at a distance. And why am I worried about it? I can get all I want without having to work for it in the village.

I pull into the parking lot, a few minutes late. I had to dance around Scott without telling him where I was going. He would have given me shit or ratted me out. But I had to borrow the car, so I told him I was headed to work on a project for school. That pissed all over his interest in going.

Quick check of the hair, breath's good. Let's have a burger.

I can see her the moment I stand up getting out of the car, but she's not alone. Through the window I can see her talking to someone, but his back is to me. She sees me and waves. He turns around and...oh. Him. But why is she with Hunter? He stands up and heads for the same door I'm going to. Is he going to hold the door for me? I get to it first, but barely.

"Hey Hunter, how's it hangin'?" But dude just brushes my shoulder walking past. What an ass.

Why did Hunter sit down in the first place? Ugh. I told him I was meeting someone. He had to be nosy. I had been dancing around answering when Trent pulled up. Then, well, Hunter could see for himself.

"Hey, sorry about that. He didn't know I was meeting you when he sat down. So, what's up?"

"Yeah, he seemed thrilled to see me. Dude sees me every day at school and won't even look my direction. Hasn't used actual words with me since two weeks ago in the park. It's cool though. You tell your mom where you were going?"

"Sharron trusts me. I told her I was meeting a friend. She just said to be safe." Josh interrupts the pleasantries to take our orders. I'm ready but Trent just got here. We ask for water.

"Must be nice. Uncle H wants to know evvvverything I do and everywhere I go. He's up my ass about everything."

"Anything I can help with? I sincerely hope your being an Eastender and meeting me isn't a problem."

"Well, I don't care about all that shit. But they do. They lecture me constantly about race and purity."

Riveting. "Race and purity? Are they living in the 1920's? What are they, Klan?"

"Probably shouldn't say this, but I do hear a lot about that around the village. There's a rumor Scott told me that the dude that's running for mayor was Klan. He seemed happy about it." I gotta change the subject. "What do you eat here?"

"Double bacon burger with cheese, chili fries, onion rings and a chocolate milkshake."

"Damn girl! You got it memorized and ready to GO! Haha. How you eat like that and keep that beautiful figure?" Ugh, you sound stupid stop talking. Thank God waiter dude is back. "I'll have what she's having." Did I really just say that?

Beautiful figure? I watch him shuffle for a moment. He didn't mean to say that. Did he not mean it? Or did it slip by accident. He's cute when he's flustered, biting that cute bottom lip. Wait, what am I thinking? Okay, I simply must know. "Beautiful figure? You checking me out?"

"I mean, yeah. But I check out a lot of girls." I'm an asshole.

What an asshole. "Really? Get around a lot, do you?"

Yeah, but things change. "No, I mean. I mean I just appreciate beauty and the female form, you know. You don't check out dudes?" Gotcha!

"I wouldn't say I 'check them out,' but I notice."

"You notice what?" Now I'm intrigued. I gotta hear this.

Damn. Make something up. Quickly, he's evaluating your honesty with every passing second. "Christopher Fitzpatrick has an amazing chest." AAAAAHHHH. What?

"Amazing chest? You're such a weirdo. Ha." Chest. How's my chest? I usually rely on my face and charm.

"I'm a weirdo? Okay Cassanova, what do you notice?" Ha!

Backed into that one. "Who the hell is Cassanova?"

"Don't you read? Answer my question."

"Ah, I can't give up all my secrets on the first date." Shit.

"Date? I thought this was just a burger. And you didn't answer my question."

"You want it to be a date? I mean you can have a burger on a date, right?"

"Answer my question please." Keep smiling. He's into it. Wait, what?

"I'll answer your question if this is a date."

"Oh is that my choice? Haha just answer? What did you notice about me?" That was not the original question.

Level. Up. "Wait, now it's about you?"

"Maybe, just ANSWER."

"DATE?"

"YES, FINE! JUST ANSWER THE DAMNED QUESTION!!"

"YOUR GLOW!" ... What did I just say?

What did he just say? Thank God. Food's here. "Thanks, Josh."

I didn't look up at her immediately. I sort of took a big bite of the burger so I didn't have to explain. But when I thought about it, it was true. She has this glow like thing around her. I mean not like an actual light, but a feeling you know? Like the closer you get the happier you feel. Then you get wrapped up in those eyes and the perfume and the hair and the smile and...

"So, other than race relations, what do you all get up to in the village?" I listen to him talk about random, ordinary things that happen that I care nothing about. I need to work through what I'm doing here. I'm in uncharted territory. I mean I am starting to like this guy, but it's bad. It's all very bad. Those people are like a cult. I don't want to be anywhere near this but...but he's different. He's not like them.

She's listening but she's not paying attention. She keeps playing with the food more than eating it and all her responses are four words or less. "What about in town? What goes on here when the cat's away?"

"Nothing really. I do school work and help out around the house. I'm pretty vanilla." Something shiny draws my attention through the glass and into the parking lot. It's Deputy's badge glinting in the sun. He comes in, takes off his hat, and pauses for a moment when he sees me. I look to Trent, who followed my eyes to Deputy. Luckily Mr. Vance can recognize an awkward situation when he sees it, so he shuffles on in and sits in a corner booth across from Sheriff Teal.

"Who's that? Your dad?"

"No. He's sort of Sharron's boyfriend, I guess. I never knew my dad." My gut reaction is to ask about his family, but I've heard his dad recently died. I don't want to bring that up. "So, what's it like changing from home to here?"

"It's not too bad. I mean I miss hunting with my dad and all back home and I miss my friends. I'd say I missed my mom but she's been in a bottle of some sort for years. There's lots of good people here though."

Good people? In the village? And Hunting? "Hunting what?"

"In Georgia we hunt deer a lot. I'm the best shot in my family, no joke. We don't just do it for sport. We eat all we kill. Keep it in the freezer. People hunt here too, right?" Surely. It's North Carolina.

"I suppose. I mean I don't. I don't think I could kill an innocent animal like that."

"Yet here you sit eating one?" Combative much?

Ugh...I put the burger down and focus on the onion rings. "That's different."

Don't say it. I want to ask different how? But I hold back. "Anyway I was a pretty good shot with my 30.06."

Charming. Change the subject. "When you say good people, do you mean you share the...views, shall we say, of the people in the village?" Ouch. Why?

"I mean, I don't buy into all of it. I ignore a lot of what they say. I just do my thing, you know?"

"And doing your thing means ignoring racism and bigotry? And people taking over our town? And intimidation in the halls at school?" I can't stop it coming out of me now. My face feels hot and I'm really getting angry. Five minutes ago he was a hot, interested guy with nice lips. Now he's pissing me off.

She's talking just like Hutch said a townie would. We aren't all racists. Or I'm not. Maybe the people in the village are but...Shit I don't know. What am I supposed to do? "What would you have me do? Take your little friend

Hunter up there to meet with Beech and see if we can all just get along? Sometimes it just is what it is."

"And sometimes you just have to tell people when they are wrong!" My voice is raising. But the anger is still coming. Now he seems weak to me. Small. Yes, that's it. Smug and small.

"AND SOMETIMES GETTING YOUR PANTIES IN A WAD DOES NO GOOD, RED!" I'm yelling. I feel a hand on my shoulder and turn to swing.

"NO!"

I stop just in time and step back. I know this dude.

"Benton. Are you okay?"

"Yes. Yes. Just checking. Checking on you. Checking on you. Okay?"

"Yes, I'm so sorry if we scared you." I step past Trent to give Benton a hug and reassure him. He seems to be satisfied. He smiles and walks away, returning his interest to his phone. "I'm sorry I yelled. I didn't mean to."

"Yeah. Me too. Maybe leave it there? Text you later?" And just like that she goes from being a snotty brat to being all tender and stuff. This girl's a lot of work. I never have to try this hard. Hell, even the lady in the office at school would jump the counter if I winked at her. But Addison Gain takes work.

Air. I need air. Space and air. Space and air and time. "Okay, maybe. If not, see you Monday?"

"Okay." God, I hope so.

BRAD

I have been a part of many goings-on in this old courthouse, but I have never left it this stunned. Sheesh. They counted the dadgum vote three times! I can't believe that friggin' bigot beat Sheriff Teal. Just goes to show you how much things really have changed around here, and mind you, not for the best.

I don't understand it. What has happened? He did not do any more or less than what he did last time around, but that village all must have voted together along with a few folks from town that maybe had met the business end of the law a time or two. It just feels like a betrayal. A John Brown betrayal. Woody Teal has been a loyal public servant in this town since before I could remember. He always does his job with steadiness and honesty with the utmost respect for the law and his department. What a crappy way to pay him back for all he had done to keep this place safe for so long. I guess in the end they just outnumber us now.

Them and us. There never used to *be* a them—only us. I don't know for the life of me why they picked Betterton, but they picked it. And now they've overrun it. It's like somebody stole something precious and you just can't get it back. Like you know who did it and you can't touch them. Makes me so stinking mad I want to just hit the friggin' gas and speed all the way to Charlotte.

Poor Woody. I've never been able to call him that before. It had always been boss, sir, or Sheriff. Now when I see him in town it will just be *Woody*. Maybe Mr. Teal. I'm not sure I could manage that. The man that hired me—that taught me how to do my blooming job—was out of a job himself. And for what? So it would go to Delbert Beecham Bethune, of all people. Made my stomach roll.

Sheriff Bethune . . . I don't much care for the taste of it coming off my tongue. How was I going to work with that guy? He has no morals, or at least ones I shared. Sheriff Teal is a humble man, an upstanding guy. It sure will be a change to be saluting and taking orders from a man I don't respect. I've never done that before. It'll be a new dadgum experience for sure. I wonder if the man knew, or cared to know, anything about the law or keeping a town safe. Heck, he'd probably not worry too much about a third of the citizens of the town. That thought sent chills down my spine.

Sheriff Bethune and Mayor Little. We might have been done for.

I turned on the cruiser and reached for my radio to check in. Then I tried Sharron again, but I didn't get her. She'd know by then. She called it. She'd said it in the morning when we went to vote and we saw who and how many were standing in the lines, early, mind you, to vote. Some regular residents probably didn't even bother. Sheriff Teal has never lost and nobody has even wanted the job of mayor. What'll he even do? The council had been doing everything. Sheesh.

Coming up on town hall on Main, I thought I saw a friendly out walking a little late tonight. I pulled up to his left and rolled down my passenger window to talk.

"Hey, Benton. You're out late tonight. Can I give you a lift?"
"Yes. Yes, sir. Just home please. Please sir."

I like ole Benton. At all the baseball or basketball games, town picnics, church services, Benton is my man. Not much to say, just plays on the phone. But he keeps me company and doesn't ask too many questions. If you need to complain, he'll listen as long as you want to talk and mind you, it never goes further than him.

"Long night?"

"Shame that vote. Vote was wrong. A Shame."

"I know, friend, I hear ya. Think how I feel, brother. I understand completely."

As I drove Benton back to his house, the one his mama left him in the will that we haven't collected taxes on in ten years, I noticed how dead the town feels. I know it's late and not many should be out, but I guess it just weighs heavier tonight than normal. What the? She shouldn't be out, it's almost ten o'clock.

"Hang on, Benton, pit stop." He just nodded and stared out the window.

"Hey, little girl, you sure are out late. Your mama know where you are? And that you're with a boy?"

"Good evening, Deputy. Yes, Sharron knows where I am and who I'm with. This is Trent. He came by and asked to go for a walk. Sharron didn't mind. Wine night."

"Ah. That explains her not answering my calls or my text when the vote was counted." "Yep. Came home and got out her grape juice. You good?"

"Yeah, I'm making it. Not too thrilled, but I'm making it. Just giving my buddy here a ride back home."

"Hey, Benton."

He looks up, but not like normal. I've never seen him talk to Addison without a smile. He's known her since she was a baby. She noticed too.

"Well, get home quick as you can. You take care of her, young man. And no funny stuff." Once the little girl was giving me daggers, Benton and I pulled away.

I hadn't noticed how much Benton's house had gone downhill. It was an old place, mind you, but it looked bad. I'll have to get over here with the men from church one Saturday and do a little work. I hopped out of the cruiser and opened my back door.

"Have a good night, Benton. See ya soon. Pleasure to be of service."

He stood up, but he didn't walk away. He had his phone in his hand so I was sure I was about to see more blurred pictures of this fall's football team or that dadgum cat he had, but it wasn't. Benton pulled up an old picture from when he and Sheriff Teal were young men. I couldn't swear it, but it was so far back it could have been Woody's first swearing in. Benton had a tear in his eye. I shook his hand and patted him on the shoulder.

"I know, brother. I know."

When I left Benton's, I probably had a tear of my own.

I think Woody will be all right. He is old enough to retire. Sheesh, I'm no spring chicken. Then my mind turns to Sharron. I hope she was sleeping well. Think I might pick her up some breakfast on my way home when the night shift ends. God, I'd love to marry that woman.

I cross the railroad tracks and cruise through the village. They are still up—lights on in every house. There are a bunch of them drinking beer and grilling out—that late. I can tell in the way they look at me, even through the glass, they think they've beaten us. Maybe they have. I am not feeling exactly steady myself, mind you.

I turn back off Fourth Avenue and head south. Coming up on the light at Main, I hear a loud engine and a horn beep twice. I pull off to the side of the road and I turn off my headlights so I'm less visible.

Out of nowhere a big white truck with a rebel flag flying from the back and mud all over the oversized tires runs the light and hangs a right on Main. Then he punches it.

I turn my headlights back on, click the noise, and light him up. He pulls over, but slowly like he might not stop. I hang back in the cruiser a minute and run the plates. I feel sure he is going to gun it, but he doesn't.

When I come up to the window for my little chat and to check the paperwork, I get a strong booze smell.

"License, registration, and proof of insurance please, sir?"

"Sure, Smokey. You got it."

"Mr. . . . Dillingham, have you been drinking tonight, sir?"

"Maybe two, Smokey, but it's been a minute. I'm fine. I got it." I didn't like the look in his eye or the arrogant attitude. We didn't know one another, which meant he wasn't from town. Didn't matter though; everyone is equal in the eyes of the law. Or at least they always have been under Sheriff Teal.

"Could you shut the engine off please and step out of the car?"

"Well, I'd rather not if it's all the same to you." Great. An idiot. Just what I need on this dadgum night.

"That wasn't a question. Turn off your truck and step down slowly. Keep your hands where I can see them." That quirky little grin and squirrely look in his eyes slowly turn into pursed lips and a scowl. But he complies.

"Mr. Dillingham, this license says you're nineteen. You realize the drinking age is twenty-one."

"It's a special occasion. And I haven't had much. There ain't no need for this shit." Sure is not a special night for me. And I have never cared for profanity.

"Sir, turn around and face the truck. Interlace your fingers behind your back." "You serious?"

"I won't ask again," I say. His eyes dart down to my hand on my weapon. Moron. I can tell for a moment he is still weighing his options. In the end he complies.

I am reading him his rights when he interrupts me. "Change is coming! Haha . . . know that, Smokey. Change is coming. Yes, sir." This coming from a drunken kid in cuffs, mind you.

"Not tonight, son." *Click*. "Not tonight." *Clack*.

10

DELBERT

They say you can't keep a good man down. Well, I guess the same could be said of a man that's been denied his destiny.

For almost twenty years a cocktail of fury and resolute determination have pulled me out of bed in the morning and driven me steadfastly through each day. It is akin to having a pair of blinders on, which keep you from being distracted or knocked off course. The naysayers, liberals, pragmatists, politically correct jerks, the opposition, the media all try to derail and deride any man that dares to speak truth to power and demand his rightful, birthright status in society. The government wants to tell you how to live. The lawyers want to tell you how to run a business. The media wants to dictate what you say. The college professors want to brainwash your children. And all of them have one purpose—a singular goal—and that is the emasculation, degradation, and displacement of the white man as a principal pillar in society. The collective power of the godless, misguided, and inherently corrupt forces, which profess to want to lead America forward, are instead marching her toward a point of no return. Perversion, subversion, and assertion of their vision of a bastardized den of mixed-race mongrels, sexual deviants, and agnostics are at the root of what is tearing this country apart. They wrap it up in a pretty package, label it progress, and pass it out to the willing, then they try to shove it down the throats of anyone who dares to disagree with them.

They worship the blacks, and the immigrants, and the Jews, and the gays. Anything but a straight white male. Nobody is standing up for our rights at all. They push women in power, gays in the military, blacks getting paid for things done to their great-grandparents, and for what? To take the white man down—to deny him religious liberties, tell him how to live, and take power from the hands in which God himself placed it in the book of Genesis. The very idea of it all propels me to stride forward and continue my crusade each day.

On this morning, however, the sun brought with it a new incitement to press on. For the first time in decades, hope is my stimulus today—an aspiration that this endeavor we have undergone will bear fruit and stand as an example to the world of a civilized, organized society as it should be. Today I stand with years of rage over being sidelined, fury over having my business destroyed, and work to right what is wrong with this nation as my foundation to stand on as I am sworn in as sheriff of Betterton, North Carolina.

I pray to the Almighty to guide me and give me the strength to endure when the mission is arduous, resolve is tested, and the sacrilegious forces of evil rise in inevitable opposition. It is for him I labor and his Word I administer. God, give me the resolve of Joshua, the patience of Job, and the wisdom of Moses.

This morning even my coffee smells magnanimous as I set it between the seats of my vehicle to proceed to the courthouse to be sworn in. It feels like preordination—destiny has brought me to this righteous post. Almost nobody left as I exit the village and proceed to what until today has been the bowels of this town. Perhaps the relative vacancy is a result of my good Christian flock wishing to stand in solidarity with me.

Some men say that life is a game of chess; moves and countermoves. As if life itself was animated and interacted with the changing wills and actions of man. In truth, life is less complicated than that. If I had to use a game metaphor, I would describe it more as an arrangement of dominos. God puts the dominos where they are destined to be. All that is required is someone motivated, inspired, spurred into righteous action to set the course in motion. The first piece fell years ago. Now, we continue our crusade with fervor and determination.

As usual, my suspicions are confirmed as an incredible, beautiful gathering of upstanding Aryan brothers and sisters has convened to witness today's patriotic and sacred event.

Cheers greet me as I emerge from my truck and stride toward the platform. I turn and acknowledge them with a humble bow and appreciative wave. Fear not, good people. You'll have stronger leadership now.

I watch politely as mayor-elect Little makes the transition to Mr. Mayor. Subsequently, each of the council members put their hands on the Bible and did their duties. Finally, it is my turn. I have asked Dewayne if I could go last today as I have a few remarks after being formally deputized.

Judge Stockman finally summons me to the podium. As I dutifully place my right hand on the Bible, I can see the unease in his eyes and smell the fear in the air. I hesitate to admit it, but it brings a smile to my face.

I comply with the customary formality of it all, making my pledge to the law and community. And then, I turn to speak.

First, I take a moment to admire the size of the crowd.

"My fellow citizens of Betterton and, more importantly, these United States, I want to thank you for coming today. I wish to be gracious in accepting the trust, which you have placed in my hands. As I said during the campaign, I will spend every waking minute ensuring that this town is secure, that our rights are properly protected, and that threats to our liberties are met with strong and decisive action.

"I have expressed to all of you, many of you personally, what my vision for Betterton was and remains. Mayor Little and I have met several times since election night a few months ago. I wish to assure you that we are on the same page, and we stand poised to lead as a team moving forward.

"Over these last few years, this municipality has been, shall we say, cloaked in an atmosphere of conflict. We have been divided, fractured by conflicting notions of what makes Betterton great. I submit to you this day that we have put the question of the trajectory of our community to the test via the election, and the community has spoken. Therefore, I take as my mandate to pursue an agenda consistent with the values and moral code of the majority of my constituents.

"Additionally, I wish to put welfare abusers, illegal foreign workers, moral and sexual degenerates, those who oppose religious freedoms and the Second Amendment, and corrupt figures in this community on notice. It is my intention to root out these sources of disharmony and moral destruction. I wish to vanquish that which is corrosive, and to nourish that which makes us stronger in the eyes of God.

"To these ends, I have several announcements which have resulted directly from my meeting with Mayor Little.

"That one, George Dillingham is to be released from the custody of the town of Betterton immediately. It is the assessment of the executive of the municipality that the initial stop and search of Mr. Dillingham's vehicle, which ultimately led to his subsequent arrest, were done improperly. It is also our finding that Mr. Dillingham was mistreated upon his arrival and has been improperly treated since his unlawful conviction in December, at which time he began his 120-day jail term.

"As a result of what in our judgment is immoral, unprofessional, and unbecoming conduct, Deputies Vance and Upchurch are hereby relieved of duty and terminated from the employment of the town of Betterton. Immediately following our gathering here, I will deputize Craig Kitchens and Edward Jackson to assist me in enforcing the laws and ordinances of Betterton.

"I wish to remind the council that as the executive of the town, Mayor Little will reassume his mayoral duties with respect to influencing the agenda of the council, enforcement of town ordinances, and allocation of funds in the town budget. His first act has been to officially veto and thereby nullify the overreaching, imposing, and ill-conceived 'Tolerance Ordinance' the council hastily and perhaps irresponsibly imposed upon citizens last year. Friends, I extend an olive branch to anyone wishing to join our noble crusade. It is my hope that a unified Betterton is a strong Betterton. But I will leave you with this: Our wills are strong, our path is clear, and our path is righteous. I ask God's blessings for all of you today and in moving forward. God bless our town, and God bless America!"

The cheers that follow serve to reassure me that my intent is fully understood, and that our first actions have been greeted with acceptance and understanding. I would invest time into persuading Vance and Upchurch to see my perspective, but what is the point when I have two perfectly capable replacements waiting in the wings?

Make no mistake about it. My feet are, as they say, taped to the bicycle. The course is set, and I have no intention of altering it in any manner. I have been contemplating, planning, and toiling for too long to lose my resolve at this crucial juncture.

In the end, it will not be me or my people who wind up eating crow.

Rumors are going around about the potential for protests in the coming days. Well, I know better than that. I am aware of who those potential redressers of grievance are, and they are not the sort to congregate in the light of day. No, sir. That sort are like rats and roaches; vermin that emerge under the cover of darkness and the protection of the night to do their dirty and unholy deeds. When the time comes, we will stand ready. We have secured the prize fairly, and we have no desire to relinquish it now. God is good.

11

REVEREND PRUITT

*L*ord, as I lay down my body for rest this evening, I wish to thank you for the blessings in my life. I do not deserve them, Lord, but I am humbly thankful that you have seen fit to bestow them on me. I ask you to please forgive me for my sins and to watch over and protect our town and this country in this our time of need. In these tumultuous days which are in store, Father, we will need you more than ever.

Lord, this night I pray for the citizens of Betterton. I pray that they be blessed with the strength to do what is right and what is righteous in your eyes, Father God. Send them wisdom and hope, love and understanding, endurance and purpose. May the good people of Betterton not be dissuaded or deterred in their faith journeys by those who preach hate and intolerance in the name of the Church. Lord, we know that Jesus preached a message of love—acceptance and embracing of that which is different from ourselves. Lord, we understand that the Church is a hospital for the sinners, not a country club for the self-righteous. Father, we know that in the words in red Jesus asks us to turn to him to calm the raging waters of the sea. That is what we seek in you.

Lord, this night I pray for the weakest among us. I pray for our minority citizens as they are surely disheartened and threatened by the words and actions of a misguided majority. I pray for those who love differently from others that they be assured that love is love and therefore should be welcomed, not condemned. I pray for our migrant workers who have sought refuge with us in search of a better life and path for their children. They are no burden, Father. We know that they help to bring nourishment to us by working the land and putting their faith in this country and in you, Father. We know that we must take the examples detailed in the Holy Gospels of Jesus standing up to injustice by those seeking power or espousing false prophecy.

Lord, finally, I pray for Mayor Little, Sheriff Bethune, and all of our new leadership. It is my sincere desire that they lay down the weapons of hate, which are used to wage unholy war against the innocent. Bring down the light of your love on them, Father. Bless them with vision to see that your will is not rooted in conflict among ourselves or abhorrence of the other. Give them guidance and make their hearts open to all of your people, Lord.

I ask these things in Jesus' name.

Amen.

12

SHARRON

The warming sensation of the cabernet cascading down the back of my tongue and careening into my body relaxes me as I settle into bed to watch television. This time of year they play the same films again and again. I do not find any of them particularly enthralling, but I shall peruse them all the same.

Christmases have not been the same since Emily died. I do not suppose that the loss of a sibling would be pleasant under any scenario, but losing a twin aged merely thirty-four years was utterly agonizing. I can close my eyes and still relish in the melody which was her laugh. A Christmas Eve from an age gone by swims to the forefront of my consciousness. Emily and I are wide awake well before daybreak, giggling in the hall, awaiting permission from our parents to proceed down the narrow corridor to the formal living room to find the bounty Santa has left us. Far from women, we are two little girls, hands clasped tightly over our mouths in an effort to muffle the sound of the excitement, trying so concertedly to ride our voices out of our bodies. Her eyes are an ashen blue, as if they have been drawn in chalk. We have on our matching pajamas, pink silk with white lace trim. We are blissfully oblivious to the fact that we are in the middle of the golden age of our lives. We allow ourselves to maintain that we will always be this way—together and happy.

The idiotic shriek of an imbecile in a car commercial pulls me from my dreamlike state and thrusts me bluntly back to the present. I cast my comforter to the floor and abandon the warmth of my bed in search of another glass of wine.

My memories of Emily are beautiful, but they never linger. Something always chases her away. One moment I could caress her warm, pink cheek with the back of my little hand, and the next she is gone, like a warm breath disappearing into a cold night's breeze.

Ten years now since breast cancer lurched my confidant from me so abruptly. Addison was only seven. It's a wonder I have succeeded in traversing my life without her. I had turned to Emily for everything. It was her who came to my rescue when I wrecked the car in high school. She was the assertive voice that warded off the bullies. Naturally, it was she who helped retrieve me from the abyss when I found myself pregnant, alone, and petrified. If I only had her to turn to now in this inexplicably tempestuous time.

The second glass is good enough to warrant a third. I carry this one from the kitchen over to the soft, colorful glow of the Christmas tree. We have fewer presents than some years past, but we have our share nonetheless. I bought a snow globe for my friend Alberta and her son, Hunter. Addison will be thrilled when she opens her new phone, and I'm sure Benton will adore the tin of sugar cookies I bake just for him each holiday season. Brad and I agreed not to exchange gifts this year in light of his current employment circumstance. He even brought up the idea of moving in here—my heart palpitates at the mere uncertainty of it all.

I have endured enough defaced barn doors, vandalized cars, and intimidated people this year to last me my next ten. I am fifty years old, and never have I seen this much disorder and unrest in this town. The likelihood of the trend-changing course seems improbable given the baboon that somehow got himself elected sheriff. God, I wish he was as dumb as he looks.

Addison has been seeing more of that boy that dwells in proximity to the unsavory elements of Betterton. Trent is a moderately respectful young man, but we would be well-served to maintain a healthy apprehension about breaching his boundaries. Friendship I can tolerate, and courtship I may suffer to endure. Nevertheless, if that little twerp gets his phallus anywhere near my child I will separate him fr

I pray for my daughter every night—before the wine, of course. I am aware that Jesus drank it. Still, I should think God would find himself most exasperated at my giggling my way through an evening devotional.

I resolve myself that tomorrow will be a merry day, full of jovial cheer, as we celebrate the end of one year and the approach of another.

I empty the bottle into my glass, turn off the tree, and follow the glow of the nightlight back to my chamber to retire. The sound of the heat kicking on startles a hiccup from me.

to find. You gotta look. And when you look you might can find nice things. I make pictures of nice things on my phone and bring them with me. I always keep them with me in my hand.

Ms. Grist always smiles. Brings my food, good food. Always smiles and always nice. Ham and potatoes. Ham and potatoes and beans. Good, good food. Mr. Jacob Grist gone to glory over a year now. He was a godly man like Mr. Teal. The cancer took him fast, fast. It's a shame, shame how something ugly can take something so kind and good, kind and good and godly. Just blew out like a candle or a dropped water glass. Gone too soon, too soon. It's a shame. And Ms. Grist all alone with only me to care for. Me and church. She plays heavenly music at the church.

I like church. Church is happy and we sing sweet music, sweet music. Makes me feel good. I got music in my phone, heavenly music. I like to hear my heavenly music. Takes away from people being ugly. Ugly people make me go inside. I can be outdoors of the house but still be inside. On my inside there's music. Music and smiles and waves and flowers, waves and flowers. I take my pictures of the waves and flowers. They wait for me on the phone when I gotta come inside.

I got the flowers in the park. The park is nice. I like nice. Some people smile and wave in the sun and the wind. I hear my music and be outside. Some people are mean and quiet, ugly and mean and quiet. Some ugly and mean and loud, real loud. Then I come indoors and inside I got my phone. I got my smiles and waves and flowers and music and it's all real nice, real nice.

And I got Ms. Gain and little Ms. Gain. I got Sheriff, I mean Mr. Teal and Reverend Pruitt and Ms. Grist and Ms. Crawford and Farmer Price. They stay here on the inside with me when they can't really be here. I got pictures of me and Mama and me and Mr. Muldune from back when I worked sweeping the mill. I miss working a lot, a lot. But I got it here on my inside to see.

It's sad to have to come inside so much. Friendly words can do so very much, so very, very much. Not friendly words can too. But I don't say. I just don't say. I just stay inside. Inside with my music and my flowers and waves and smiles.

13

BENTON

I'm not going not going. Not going at all. They s'pose I don'
know, but I do. I do. They wanna make trouble. I don't like
trouble, trouble is bad, bad. Outdoors tonight might be trouble.

They s'pose I don't see but I see. I see, I see and hear. I know
People been talking loud. Loud and mean. Mean. Guess the
say what they think. Think it fine. But saying it, saying it can b
bad, just bad. I think a lot, but I don't say. I don't say what I'
thinking good like everybody. I just keep it inside, inside don
hurt nobody so I keep it inside. But I know. I see and I know.

I see the change. Change can be bad, bad. Been two month
since Sheriff Teal is just Mr. Teal. That's a bad change, a re
bad change. Good man. Godly man. Friendly man, friend
I know Woody my whole life, my whole entire life. He's a kin
man and he smiles and waves a lot. Shame that vote. Sham
shame. Sheriff Teal ran a friendly town. Friendly town wi
friendly people who smiled and waved.

I like a friendly town. Smiles and waves and flowers and t
wind. Nice things. Nice things are hard to find here now. Ha

I s'pose I'll put my plate in the sink. Ms. Grist says she'll pick it up tomorrow. I might sit and watch my programs. Ms. Grist is a good woman. A godly woman.

Ms. Grist told me stay in tonight. Tonight might get real bad, real bad. I heard at church. At church, they talk about being mad and going outside mad. Say they might be outdoors mad all together making noise and getting in some trouble. I don't like trouble at all, at all. Some folks at church don't like the bad, bad change. They not takin' to the new sheriff at all, at all. Mr. Teal say to be calm, but it's too much ugliness going on, too much. They say they got to fight back. I don't like to fight. I like smiles and heavenly music like on my phone and on my programs.

I'll stay indoors clear of trouble and watch my programs. My programs don't come on TV no more so I use the box. Ms. Gain brought the first box two years ago. I got a new box from her last month for Christmas. Ms. Gain is a good woman. A godly woman. The box keeps my programs for when I have to stay in at night. On tonight I ain't going nowhere, nowhere.

It's noisy outdoors tonight. I s'pose they out there making trouble and getting mad. Ugly and mad. I look out the glass and see folks walking hard and looking real mean, real mean. I don't understand why it is this way. Why can't we just smile and wave and enjoy the flowers and be nice? Just say sorry and be nice?

I don't want this at all, at all. I'll just stay indoors and pull up my programs and turn up TV. I'll just turn it up. If that don't work, I'll go back inside with my phone. Inside with waves and flowers and smiles and heavenly music. Help it all, God. Help it all.

SCOTT

These sore losers have been spoiling for a fight since the night Beech and Twig Little won elections they thought they had in the bag. I tell ya, man, they have been pissing and moaning around town, shooting us dirty looks at school, even getting in shouting matches with some of us at the gas station or Spires' Grocery.

I understand why Daddy calls them snowflakes. These jokers can complain about anything! Before we all heard the comments about racism and homophobia and all that crap. Which, to tell you the truth, I didn't really have that big of a deal with. I mean, they're partly right. I do prefer to surround myself with my own kind. I'll give them that one. But I don't like the term *homophobic*. It makes it sound like I'm scared of them or something. I'm not scared—I just don't want to be around the nasty bastards.

Now, they complain about the new deputies not doing regular patrols on Main and some of the residential streets. They're claiming that Eastenders are stealing things from their yards or garages and damaging property without fear of the police. I say, hey! We know how to take care of our property, man. I got a high-speed, wireless device for that. And I got the bullets to put in it. I tell ya, if you didn't spend so much time railing against your own Second Amendment rights, you could handle your own.

They whine about Mayor Little and Sheriff Bethune taking the reins and bringing some control and stability back to this town. They show up at council meetings crying about the new taxes they came up with to help rebuild the old mill to bring jobs back to Betterton. They don't like our flags or our hats or our loud trucks. I tell ya, man, these jokers could complain about a bright blue sky, I swear.

It all boils down to one little fact that they will not admit to. They can't stand it that a disciplined white man has the guts to stand up and be proud of his heritage. Period. And they really lose their minds when one of us is in charge and running things. Now we have two men like that in Beech and Twig, and they flat can't stand it, man. It's that simple.

For months we have been listening to crap day in and day out everywhere we go in town. But tonight is a new ballgame. They've poked the fire ant mound one too many times and now they're about to really get stung! We've all seen and shared the posts going all around social media about the "peaceful demonstration" they've planned to protest the new order here in town. Well, I tell ya, this Georgia boy and his fellow crusaders have got something for them, and it ain't a pillow to bite on. And how stupid can they be? All their posts are public! Me and Hunter McMillan have been commenting back and forth to one another for three days. I mean they have to know we know! I told that boy I'd like to catch him alone one good time. All he could come up with was "bring it, white boy." You think I see white as a weakness? I swear I hate him.

Either way they have to expect us to respond. Do any of us boys seem like the type to back down from a fight? Beech told us he had a plan, and I tell ya, man, I believe him.

Now, we aren't stupid. We know better than to start the whole crap storm. Right now we are all just sitting tight, cookin' supper, keeping in touch with snaps and texts, just being cool. They don't know we are ready with a counterprotest. We have our own bullhorns and cowbells to drown them out. And if that won't work, Twig told us to chant, "Law and order! Law and order!" Some of my friends and neighbors seem a smidge nervous. Not me. I'm ready. I have been waiting on something to snap this tension so we can get back at them for the lies and the complaints for months. I am practically chomping at the bit to set this sucker off!

The sun is well into disappearing over the horizon. The sky goes from yellow to orange to blood red. I'm in the middle of wondering whether I should get a flashlight or just use the darkness to my advantage when it comes—the message from our neighbor and family friend Albert Connoley that they've organized down around the diner and seem to be headed east on Main toward town hall.

"Let's go, boys!" Mr. Ivey yells. "Let's fight fire with fire! *But remember what Beech said! Do not forget it.*"

I estimate we number about forty or fifty men and older boys leaving First Avenue passing by the mill. We hang a left and head toward town hall as well coming from our side of the tracks. My blood is pumping and my fists are tight. I'm so ready I can't stop licking my lips in anticipation. I keep thinking, *Come on. Come on and get here. I got something for ya, man. Come on. Come on!*

At first, we don't see them because of the little hill leading up to where you cross the tracks. We hear them though. At first, it sounds really muffled and I can't quite make out what they are saying. Then it gets clearer and clearer, *Equal rights and equal treatment! Equal rights and equal treatment!*

The sun is just dipping below the line and the cool night air bites my nose as my hot breath reaches the air along with my other crusaders. *Law and order! Law and order! Law and order!*

Even though the air is cold, my blood is running hot. And I'm not alone, I tell ya. Man, everybody feels like we are marching as a unit—like we are all part of one animal bigger, stronger, more ready than they are—itching to flex our muscles and put these little pissant shits back in their box once and for all!

We cross the tracks and come down the hill right toward them. We all meet up in the intersection of Main and Old Mill Road. We do like Beech said and stop about five feet in front of them. I'll be damned if the first one I see isn't McMillan. He sees me too. We hold each other's eyes like we can't let go. I wish Beech would just turn us loose. I'd like to knock that fake mean look right off of his face. He looks hungry too. I want him bad.

Law and order! Law and order!

Equal rights and equal treatment! Equal rights and equal treatment!

We chant back and forth for what seems like five minutes, but it's probably only a few seconds when someone on their side is heard shouting something different into the crowd. I halfway hear it, but I am not losing my focus on this one.

"*Easy!* Easy! Now we all know that our protest is peaceful. *Peaceful!* Now these people have come for a fight. We will *not* give it to them. *But* we will not cower in the face of opposition either." I hear Fin Fetter's voice more clearly as the crowds both strain to hear what's happening.

"We ain't here for no fight, son. But we ain't taking no disrespect to our duly elected sheriff and mayor like this lying down! You can take that to the *bank!*" I hear Clancey Adams yell. Heck, his family ain't been here more than a few months, but I like him.

McMillan's fists are balled up too. Wonder if his fingernails are eating into his palms like mine are.

"All we want is equal treatment under the law! You know, the constitution!?" What the hell? They got girls with them? That's the Gain chick Trent likes so much.

McMillan's leg twitches and I cock my head to one side, itching to pull the trigger. My arms are tingling from adrenaline and clenched fists.

"You would get it too if you would stop betraying your race and your *God!*" Biscuit Dillingham sounds as ready to go as I am.

The few men in the middle keep yelling over the noise, but the chants come back.

Law and order! Law and order!

Equal rights and equal treatment! Equal rights and equal treatment

I can't take it anymore. I hear Beech's words, but every bone in my body is ready to explode.

"Whatcha got, white boy?" I hear him yell. For a split second, I close my eyes and roll my head once around from shoulder to shoulder. In that instant, I hear nothing. The entire world goes stone silent for one breath.

I open my eyes and I've already closed the space that had been between us. The first shot is dead center to the nose and *damn*, it feels good. He starts swinging back, but I can't feel it. Three or four body shots land on him before he finally catches my eye. As he's drawing his arm back, I jump and plant my forehead right in the middle of his face again. When I look up, I can see him staggering backward, holding his face.

A huge force pulls me away, but I lurch. I can't break free, but I give it all I have. I recover the vision in both eyes clearly, and I can see he's not advancing either. He's being pushed deeper into his crowd. All of the men from the middle on our side are lined up facing us, trying to back us up. *"No! Remember what Beech said! Back up! Back up!"*

I take a breath and look around. My surroundings come back into focus, and all reason seems to return. That's when I hear the diesel engine behind us. I turn and see a big truck with the water cannon on top coming down the hill over the railroad track. Beech said he had a surprise hidden in the mill, but we didn't know what it was. He wanted to keep it quiet in case it wasn't needed and could stay secret.

Right behind him and pulling off to each side of him are Jackson and Kitchens on cycles in full gear. Our crowd immediately disperses and gets behind the line. Two more men from the village, Connoley and Frank Lee, flank the deputies.

Before the other side could try to explain, Beech started spraying left to right with the cannon. The deputies set off flash bombs just in front of the crowd while Lee and Connoley started unpinning tear gas canisters and hurling them in every direction at the townies.

I can hear the screaming and shouting and confusion and it's absolutely delicious. I feel a hunger sort of satisfied inside my gut. It feels like a sweet release at last. Feel it. Feel the fire, you bastards!

As I watch them scatter in every direction and hear the sound of the water die down, I take a moment to take in as big of a breath as I could. I wanted my lungs full of the air that was pierced the night we showed them down and made them run. It's bitter cold but tastes like pure honey.

One last glance at the wet streets with the teargas hovering above the empty streets, and I head back to the village, my chest bursting with pride. This is our town.

ADDISON

The *beep-beep-beep* of yet another moving truck brings my nightly beauty rest to an abrupt end. Since relatively nothing has changed in Betterton in the month or so since our protest-turned-riot, several families have opted to just put their houses on the market and get out—a few before the homes even sold.

Last night around nine or so I closed my bedroom door, cut the volume to my phone, and worked on Ms. Oberry's spring term paper until I almost fell asleep at my desk. The woman has quite the reputation for ripping papers to shreds with her little red pens because she has little else to do with her weekends. She's a nice enough woman, but her writing assignments can be brutal. After finishing the last citation, I closed my laptop and stumbled into bed. I was out like a light until the beeping commenced.

The cool room is not an inviting alternative to the warmth of my bed just yet. After a good full-body stretch, I take a sip of water and reach for my phone.

What the heck? Why do I have fourteen missed calls overnight? I'm awake now. A swipe right and a thumbprint lead me to find that I also have twenty-plus missed texts and more app notifications than I can process.

Something has happened, but I have no clue at all what it might be. I decided to start with the texts. The first conversation I pull up is from Jenna Upchurch, and it only says, *Isn't this awful!* What? Isn't what awful? Details, Jenna! Next came one from Francisco Alvero, president of our Spanish Club. *I can't believe Hunter would do it. I mean it's just not like him at all.*

DO WHAT?

I go instinctively to my conversation with Hunter, which we have had going since we learned to text. Nothing since yesterday when I told him I was about to work on my paper. I call but it goes straight to voicemail.

I call Francisco on speaker phone and pull up Facebook as I listen to three rings. Hunter's Facebook is locked.

"Bueno? Hello? Addison? I—"

"Francisco, I have heard nothing. I don't know anything. For the love of God, just tell me what is happening and how it involves Hunter?"

"Oh. You haven't heard?" OMG!

"No! That's why I am asking! What is it?" I'm trying to control the tone of my voice, but I have trouble knowing if I'm successful. He stays silent for a moment. All I can hear is the ceiling fan and a few seconds tick off from the clock on the wall.

"Okay, okay. Look, some *mierda* went down last night on Facebook."

"What? I can't see anything. Hunter's is disabled or turned off or something." "*Estoy seguro.* They might be freezing it for evidence or something."

"Evidence? Of what? Francisco, make some sense!" I have abandoned the effort at voice control.

"Okay, you remember that thread from last month between him and that Eastender dude? The one he got in the fight with right before all hell broke loose?"

"Yeah, that's Trent's cousin. What about him?" My mind is shooting in twenty different directions as I try to search Trent's contacts on his profile trying to find Scott. Nothing.

"Well, last night they got into it again. There was comments everywhere. They were way extra! Like *'I gotchu when I see you, coon!'* And *'One on one any day, white boy'* back and forth over and over. And people were egging them on like *cabrones* making it worse and worse."

"Yeah? And?" Get to what happened in *real life*!

"Well, they both went offline. I thought the conversation was *terminada pero*, it wasn't. Like thirty minutes later I start getting all these texts and snaps and mierda about *los dos*. All I know is that Scott dude is dead, and they pinched Hunter for it . . ."

The sentence hangs in the air. My mouth is moving, but nothing will come out. It's like for a moment nothing works. My hands won't move, my voice refuses to come on, and my mind goes from racing to stunned silence.

"Hello? Addie?"

"Hunter's been arrested?"

"Yeah. Somebody at the bowling alley heard a gunshot and called the law. That Jackson guy was on duty. He got there and dude was dead. *Mi primo* Angel was eating at the diner and came out *cuando vio las luces azules*. He saw the cop pointing his gun at Hunter's car and shouting. He said Hunter got out with his hands up, faced the other way, and got on his knees. Then I guess the cop was mad and slammed his face into the parking lot when he was arresting him. Then the new sheriff—*¿Cómo se llama?*—he showed up. Then more cops. I don't know from there."

A car door slams, footsteps in the carport, the back door, Sharron.

"I gotta go, Francisco. I'll text you later." I don't wait for his response. Phone in hand, I make my way down the hall through the den and to the kitchen.

"Mom, I—" She brushes past me to put two bags of groceries and her purse on the counter by the stove.

"I know, I just heard. At the store, Cameron Spires told me. I don't know much, but I have to call Alberta." She fumbles for her phone in her bag. When her hand finds it, she wastes no time.

"Okay, okay. McMillan . . ." She finds the contact information, calls the number, puts the phone to her face, and waits.

"Alberta? It's Sharron Gain."

I can't help myself. "Mom, ask if he's okay! Please!" My voice is breaking. That must mean I'm crying. She strains to hear and tries to stop me with her hand.

"Just please ask, Mom!" I know she has to, but I can't help getting a little mad when she steps into her bedroom and closes the door behind her.

I can hear her talking a little through the door, but I can't understand. I mostly hear silence as she listens. My God, I have long thought of this as a war, but I never thought people would actually die.

I go back to the living room and start to wring my hands and pace. Hunter? A killer? You'd have to be clinically insane to buy that. I mean I know he hated Scott and all the rest of the Eastenders. Trent included. But murder? There's no conceivable way that's possible. God, I wish I had a cigarette.

The doorknob snaps me back to the present as Mom steps out. Her face would have been almost unreadable if the eyes didn't give away the worry and anxiety racing through her.

"Addison, sit down."

She sits with me and collects herself.

"It's not good. Alberta said the police found Hunter sitting in his car with his hands on the wheel. When they got him out, he had blood on his hands and his shirt. The officer said he resisted."

"That's NOT what Francisco's cousin said he saw!"

"Let me finish. That's what they told Alberta and Sam. That's what is in the police report. The State Bureau of Investigation still has the parking lot of the school roped off. Classes are canceled for Monday. Hunter is in custody. I'm afraid he can't get before Judge Stockman until at least Tuesday. She was worried about how he was being treated by Bethune and his men. She did say the state police were still interviewing him when she got down to the station. She said she told them they couldn't talk to him without her or an attorney. Since there are no lawyers in Betterton because the only two we had moved away, they sent for someone from the Public Defender's office in Cumberland County. I guess someone will come to talk to him today. I don't know with today being Saturday."

"But . . . but he can't have . . ." The dam bursts. Sharron pulls my head to her shoulder and lets the tears soak into her sweater for a moment. I can smell her perfume as I listen to her take a deep breath, then let out a sigh. She gently pulls me away by the arms and looks knowingly into my eyes. "Of course not. I have known Hunter since the day Reverend Pruitt baptized him. I don't believe him capable of such a thing, not even in self-defense. I need to call Brad. I'll be right back." She retreats to her room. I want to text Trent, but surely their family is in shock. I'm not even sure he'd want to talk to me right now.

I swipe my phone again and find my own profile. It doesn't take long to find Hunter's face smiling beside mine in my pics. I can't stop staring. Crying and staring. How could this be? How? I put the pillows to my ears and let myself fall slowly to the middle of the sofa. The soft cushion muffles my scream.

ALBERTA

Dear Diary,

Thirteenth of February.

My hands were trembling when I reached to pull you down from the shelf this evening. Now, I find myself clutching this pen so hard that I may very well break it. I never thought I would have to use the words *my child* and *incarcerated* in the same breath, but that is where you find me today.

Sam seems to me to be in a state of shock, almost numb with confusion and anxiety. He answers questions, but he does not ask them. I know he is aware of what is happening, but he seems unable to interact with the goings-on of the day. I only remember my husband this way after his mother and father passed. I love him, but I confess to you that he is not much help or comfort to me in this state. Still, I must leave him to cope in his way just as I shall in mine.

I will, however, express to you what is in my heart today. I wish I could narrow my emotions down to one or two, but I am filled with so many that it seems as though they are fighting for space in my very soul.

I am frustrated tonight. Frustrated at a justice system that keeps a child who has just witnessed unspeakable acts in a cage without regard to his mental or physical condition. Frustrated that the only lawyer sent by Cumberland County is about as competent as a minister who has not known a relationship with Jesus. Frustrated that my child's life, and therefore my own, hangs in the balance and seems to be swimming rapidly out of control. Frustrated that first people could not see the evil seeds that had been planted when those people began to come. Frustrated that when they did see, they did not do. They did not *do* anything to stop the flood of unspeakable hatred invading our shared space. Frustrated that when they finally wanted to *do* something, it was too late. The seeds had become a powerful, living force that is now pressing upon all of us.

How convenient and comforting it must be to wake up white. To have the privilege to regard the oppression of minorities as a somewhat important, what's the word . . . abstract issue worthy of debate, but not imperative enough to warrant action.

Frustration gives way to confusion. I become utterly confused. Why did he go to that place? Was his intention really to fight that boy? Why hadn't he simply done as he has been instructed to do and let his father and I know of any threat made to someone in this house? Why didn't someone, anyone from that Facebook, call my home and let us know that a conflict had been in the making in broad daylight? Mostly, why do people allow hatred and ignorance so steadfastly that a mess like this is even a possibility?

Confusion advances to anger. I am thoroughly . . . indignant first and most ardently with my son. It may be true that outside parties influenced him, incited him, and motivated him to react. But the fact of the matter remains that Hunter made unwise and downright foolish choices that go against everything he has been taught. I am angry with myself because as his mother I should have known, should have seen or sensed that something was about to happen. Further, I am on the cusp of rage at the lack of control both Sam and I seem to be able to exert over the entirety of the situation. It is beyond expression the feeling of trying to run in an ever-expanding and rising pool of water that shows neither compassion nor signs of receding. I close my eyes and hang my head at the mere weight of it all.

I just want to go back to Thursday. Life was good Thursday. I knew who I was and where I was going. I had hope for my baby, strength in my husband, and faith beyond doubt. Now, like in a dream, my world feels taken, stolen from me in these last few earthly hours.

I pray to Father God for the wisdom to navigate this storm, to walk through this valley. My friend and church sister Sharron is trying to contact a civil rights attorney from Raleigh. I hope he is a godly man. An answer to the most sincerest prayers I have ever lifted to him. Protect my child from the evil forces that seek to destroy all that is good in this town and its people.

Deliver my baby, dear God. Bring my baby home to me. Amen.

Alberta

EDDIE

The smell of chicken frying means supper ain't too far off. My wife may not be the best housekeeper that ever lived, but she can flat put a scald on a bird.

Emma's got the windows all flung open trying to get some fresh air in here. Spring's her favorite time of the year. I don't mind it much myself—means February is done. *Black History Month*. I hated when Melvin came home with that crap every year back in Kentucky. *"Read about this one"* and *"Write a paragraph about that one."* Got on my frappin' nerves.

They don't even teach these kids that March is Irish-American Heritage month, but every year come February you can't get away from all the bleeding hearts yapping about how wonderful *they* are. I think I'll pop open a cold one and see what's hassling with the Pro Bass Tour.

I loved to fish when I was a boy back in Kentucky—out on the water, early in the morning with a hot cup of coffee and the smell of the pines. I swear I never felt closer to God than when I was wetting a hook.

Melvin ain't much for fishing. The onliest thing he cares about a catfish is whether it's plain fried or salt and peppered. His granddaddy though, the one he's named for, now that sucker loved it.

My old man put me in the boat with him every chance that come round. I seen more of him on the pontoon than I did at the house. He wasn't much for talking at home or at work in the mine, but if you was to get him out in nature, on his own, he'd tell ya all you needed to know. We talked about life, and God. He spoke about what it meant to be a good man; not just as a person but as a Christian, a husband, and a patriot of this country. He believed in taking pride in who you are and being proud of where you come from. He passed away from a heart attack six weeks before my boy was born.

I made the old man a promise the day we put him in the ground. I swore to him that my child would grow up to know the same kind of values and pride as I had, even though he wouldn't be there to help me. I hope he'd be proud of the job me and Emma done.

Here lately every time I think of my own son, I can't help but to feel terrible for poor Hutch Inman. I can't imagine what him and Iris are going through. I mean, to have your boy taken from you like that must be just awful.

We still ain't worked out who all was involved on the night in question, though I'm sure the gaps will get filled in as time passes. Beech has a unique way of tying things up nice like even when some pieces might not be accounted for.

We are aware about the fight on the internet, and we know that boy either killed Scott or set him up to be killed. His messages pretty much confessed to him wanting to cause Scott harm, but he couldn't have done it on his own. Scott would not have just walked up on somebody carrying a big riffle, and you can't just hide a 30.06. Besides, the weapon itself was not found at the crime scene, and McMillan never left there after the shooting. We haven't located it yet. Somebody had to get away with it, but we haven't been able to figure out exactly who it is at this point. And that Hunter kid hasn't cracked not one bit. He won't budge from his version of the event.

We'll nail him down though. He may not have pulled the trigger, but he may as well have. His words and actions that night led Scott to that schoolhouse and cost him his life. He'll pay for it, of that I can assure you. We'll either find out who helped him and how, or Beech will *decide* those facts himself. It pays to be *Sheriff* Bethune.

I just wish the State Bureau hadn't jumped in the mix so damned fast. At first they just sent us some backup units and a crime scene processor. Now Beech says he's hearing whispers and whatnot about a possible takeover of the whole investigation. We'll do all we can to put a stop to it, I'll tell you that.

Emma breaks my train of thought. "Supper will be ready in about ten minutes, hon. You want to text Melvin and see where he's at? Tell him Clinton is welcome too. I got enough."

"All right, sugar. I'll shoot him a line." I text a quick *"y'all come and get it!"* to my boy. Him and Clinton are probably out in the county somewhere burning up gas in the new truck I got for him. She's a beauty, I tell ya. Cost a pretty penny too, but working for Beech, well, it does come with its perks here and there.

I get up and walk to the window facing the road in front of the house. It's getting warmer out there, and the days are getting longer. I can smell the pollen in the air thick as butter on a biscuit.

I can just make out the Inman place from here. Wonder what the mood is like over there tonight. Can't be good. If it was me, the onliest thing I'd be able to think about would be getting justice for my boy.

I still can't figure out why the damned townies felt like they actually had to kill one of us. I mean, we all figured they'd try to fight back after their little *protest* didn't go like they planned, but nobody thought they'd go this far. Those dang liberal race traitors are usually not real aggressive when the rubber actually meets the road. They talk a good game about their *values* and their leftist, *politically correct* bullcrap, but they ain't much for backing up all that talk with action.

It's going to backfire on them, though. You watch it. They've very clearly showed the difference between our decent Christian way of life and their animalistic tendencies. It ought to be perfectly clear to the rest of the world outside Betterton who is in the right and who is not here.

I see my boy pulling in the drive and let his mama know him and Clinton's made it back. After I cut off the TV, I head into the kitchen and kiss my bride on the cheek. I hear laughter as the door opens.

I yell out to them, "Y'all get up to much today, fellas?"

Melvin takes his hat off as he makes his way into the kitchen, "No, sir. We just went for a spin after school let out. Just rolled down the windows, listened to some music, and took in that good ole country air."

"I like it," I tell him with a proud papa smile. "It's good for a man to get out in nature every once in a while. It helps clear your mind of all the bullcrap of everyday living."

Emma chimes in, "Boys, y'all wash up and get ready. I'm setting everything down at the table now."

I'm the first one to sit down and see this spread my bride has laid out for us. Fried chicken, deviled eggs, macaroni and cheese, cornbread, rolls, and green beans. We're gonna eat good tonight, I'll tell you that. Once we're all at the table, and the food's been blessed, I ask the boys about their day.

"What'd y'all get into at school?" I ask, pulling the skin off a chicken thigh and putting it in the middle of a roll.

"Nothing much. Mrs. Lewis started the day like she always does with her little inspirational quotes about unity. Today's was something from Martin Luther King," Clinton informs me.

"Why? It's March? Nobody told her we're done with that crap for a while?" I fire back. I have to wash down my last bite with some sweet tea before I finish my thought. "You kids should not have to be subjected to that liberal crap all year round. It's fine, we gave them their little month, but it's over now."

Melvin takes a mighty hunk off of a chicken leg and says, with his mouth full, "I know, Dad. I reckon she's just trying to keep things peaceful. She ain't got to worry about that, though. She ain't the one in charge of keeping the peace no more. Not really."

I can tell by Emma's face that she don't like that. Sure enough she tells him, "Now don't talk like that at the table. And don't go acting the fool at school neither. The last thing we need around here is to give them another reason to whine and complain about us. Pass the butter, please, Clinton baby."

"I know, Mama. We ain't going to do nothing unless they start it first. They won't though. They're scared we'll beat the crap out of them if they try anything," says Melvin. I gotta admit, I'm right proud of him sounding like a grown man who ain't afraid to stir up a little dust if necessary.

Clinton grabs a piece of warm cornbread and adds, "Well, they're right about that one, ain't they!" The both of them start to laugh. Emma wipes the smile off my face with the look in her eyes. I have to remind them, "Fellas, fellas. Cool it, now. Melvin, your mama's right. Don't do a thing that's going to make that woman call me down to that schoolhouse. I'm a deputy now and I don't need folks thinking I don't even have control over what my own son gets mixed up in at school."

"Yes, sir," he mumbles, pouring himself a second glass.

Emma puts the matter to bed, at least for now. "We ain't making this about us. This is about what happened to Scott and who is going to have to answer for it. We can't forget that."

Oh, somebody's gonna answer for it, I'll tell you that runs through my mind, but I don't let it come out of my mouth.

Melvin changes the subject. "Those new folks' kids came for their first day today. They seem all right."

"Which ones? The Wickers or the Nelsons?" I ask, reaching for another thigh. I know I shouldn't, but this is one tasty yard bird.

Clinton answers as Melvin's mouth is too full of macaroni to make words. "The Nelsons. They said their dad seen an ad about us on some website. Next thing you know he called Beech—"

My bride cuts him off. "*Sheriff* Bethune, please."

"Yes, ma'am. Next thing you know he called Sheriff Bethune and they made arrangements to move here, just like that. Said it happened real quick like."

Now I can't fight the smile on my face if I tried. The onliest thing I can say to that is, "Well, boys, I expect we might see a little more of that around here. I expect we just might." Nobody asks any questions about that. Everyone just turns back to their meals and makes small talk until Emma starts clearing dishes. I give her another kiss on the cheek and tell her, "That sure was good, sugar. It really was."

"Thank you, hon. I'm glad you liked it. Hey," she nods for me to come closer to her at the sink.

"Yeah, sugar, what is it?" I whisper.

"Now you don't need to be amping them up, hon," she warns with a worried look on her face.

"They're just kids, sugar. They're blowing off steam at home 'cause they can't at school, that's all," I try to reassure her.

"Well, just be careful. With that McMillan boy's trial pending, I don't want no trouble. Y'all do have that under control, right?" she asks.

My smile comes back as I declare, "Yeah. We got this one, I'll tell ya that."

SEÑOR VALDEZ

Waving goodbye to the last few students leaving in their cars brings a welcome yet bittersweet end to this school year. There is no greater reminder of the deafening disharmony of this school year than the light-colored area of pavement in the student parking lot where Fernando tried to pressure wash away Scott Inman's blood. The thought of what the scene must have been like, along with the hot air out here, sends me back inside more hurriedly than normal.

I take in a long, deep breath of wonderful air-conditioning as my eyes readjust from the bright, hot parking lot to the inner sanctum of the school. It smells like cleanser and markers in here. I have taught at this school for nine years, and I have never waited for the month of May nearly as much as this one. I check my phone briefly on my way back to secure my classroom for the summer and gather what little I will be taking with me.

Happily, I will not be spending this summer in Betterton. My family owns a resort in Panama, and I teach English courses over the summer for local university students. Two hours of *Hello. My name is Edgar. I am a student. Where is the bathroom, please?* each morning allows me to enjoy the gym, beach, and other amenities offered in and around the hotel. I had considered making the change permanent this year, but after careful consideration decided to return in the fall. I only pray that I do not live to regret it.

The classroom gets one last once-over glance as I switch off the lights and head to the cafetorium. Each year the entire district convenes here for our end-of-the-year meal and Teacher of the Year awards. It's their way of telling us they really appreciate what we do, but not enough to give us a bonus.

"You headed down now, Mat?" Mrs. Lewis calls from behind as I lock my door.

"Yes, ma'am. I'm on my way. I just have to turn in my laptop with Regina. You need me to grab anything from the office for you?" I'm not a kiss-ass, but I do try to be helpful.

"Oh no, I'm all set. I found your contract on my desk. I can't tell you how glad I am that you'll be back with us next year. See you in there!" She pats my elbow and goes on down the hall.

I really do like Nancy. In fact, I really like teaching— especially in this school. One could probably argue that my affection for this place and my concern for the students here make contemplating leaving so painful. Betterton has generally been a happy, light-hearted place full of pleasant students eager to learn and a faculty that is quite glad to come to work every day. It's only the past eighteen months or so that have seen such a shift in the atmosphere here. The tension in the halls, even sometimes in the lounge, has been palpable. We are not used to having fights or hearing racial slurs at lunch or during the changing of classes. We certainly are not accustomed to having students shot in the head after hours in the parking lot.

I almost mindlessly place my laptop in the vault for the summer, manage a smile at Regina, and slink down to the cafetorium where a meal from the Finer Diner awaits me. The halls seem so bare with all the students' work taken down. The echo of my feet from the shiny, polished floor to the painted brick walls is strangely calming—predictable and steady, if nothing else.

I see an open seat between Chris Charles and Brian Mercer. I smile and give obligatory *I'll miss yous* to anyone who manages to catch my attention along my way. Finally, I reach my destination just in time for a quick *hello* before Nancy begins to quiet the room for our greeting. Mrs. Lewis offers us a call to welcome, then Mayor Little offers a prayer that finds more eyes rolling than closing in reverence. Finally, it's time to line up for a heart attack on a plate and a glass of iced tea.

I hear the conversations as we cue up for a greasy fried chicken and lumpy mashed potatoes. They're all buzzing about the election last year, the march turned riot in January, and of course, Hunter McMillan. That poor kid has been sitting in jail for three months awaiting trial for a crime that I'm sure he can't have committed. I remember him fondly from class and from the basketball court. Such a nice kid. It's a shame really. Even if he does manage to clear his name, his life is still forever altered.

When we regain our places at the table, the conversation turns to taxes. Mr. Charles can't believe that property levies are higher with no pay raises for teachers. Brian registers an opinion, but I'm only half listening as I peel the skin off of my chicken breast and set it off to the side of my plate.

I keep telling myself to smile and be pleasant. In two days I'll be on a flight to paradise and school will be ages away.

Mr. Norton, one of our science teachers, is crowned Teacher of the Year. I make my way after the official adjournment to shake his hand and offer congratulations before hitting the door and going straight for my car.

For the first time in my career, I drive away thrilled to have the school in my rear-view mirror.

SALLY

It's awfully hot and still out here today. Even for July weather, this is most disagreeable, but I can't leave. Not quite yet.

Reverend Pruitt did a lovely job with the eulogy. Hard to believe it, but half of Betterton turned out to bid farewell to Benton Augustus Wilson. Godspeed to a man who was born different, lived a life more honest and decent than anyone I have ever known, and was fortunate enough to go home to his mother and to God peacefully as he slept.

Of course, he had no living relatives as I am aware, but he had his fair share of mourners. Everybody is gone now except me. I'm sitting here in Betterton Gardens trying to get my thoughts together. I suppose I should head on too, but something holds me here for just a little longer. My heart feels like he's still here until the entire funeral is over, and if I don't leave this bench, it can't quite be over.

Just this Friday last I was taking Benton's supper by, roast and carrots, one of his favorites. We talked about life and the weather, not much really. I told him I was glad summer seemed to have had a calming effect on Betterton. Perhaps that was because the children were out and not forced into unfamiliar groups at school. But who knows? Benton was asking about my flower bed and whether or not I needed him to come by and see to my begonias. He was always the helpful sort. Even when he wasn't lending a hand, he was nice to spend time with. You don't really appreciate having willing ears around until you haven't any.

Benton came into my life when his mother Birdie came to work for Jacob and me in our home. She was a terribly shy, but a loyal and hardworking young woman from the start. She mostly made prudent choices in life. She was forced to tell me, through tears, about one decision she very much regretted at the time. Although it all turned out for the better when Benton came along. I thought she'd struggle having a child that was so special, but she was a natural-born mother through and through. The landlord she was renting from in the mill village kicked her out for being pregnant and unmarried, so Jacob and I moved her into one of our guest rooms until Benton was six months old. After that she moved into a little property Jacob acquired, I gathered, just to rent to her on the cheap. When she died, well, we just gave the little place to Benton. It wasn't worth all that much, but she didn't leave him two red pennies to rub together. She minded her bank account all right; there just didn't ever seem to be much of it. She always had a little too much month at the end of the money, though she wouldn't ask for a cent. We always figured out a way to help her make ends meet. After all, by the time Benton was two, she was like a sister to me, and he was the child I could never have.

Now here I am laying him to rest right beside his mother and my husband. There's only me now. I suppose God still has more for me to do, maybe someone else to look after. But that's a worry I'll have to chew on another time.

A gentle wind disturbs the tall oaks like a slight whisper from heaven. The air cools my face and points out the perspiration on my brow and the tear on my cheek. It sort of feels like Benton nudging me to move on.

I walk beneath the awning and approach the disturbed earth. I laid down a begonia, a prayer, and a few tears.

"I'm going to miss my Benny boy. You be good to Jacob and Birdie. You tell them I'll be along in time. Be sure and come find me when I do so we can all be together again. I love you, my dear. I love you very much."

I have to gather myself to head back to the car before I sink back down on that bench. It's a short, quiet, somber ride home. I don't think I've been in a car this quiet in all my life.

The newspaper is waiting for me on the porch as I begin to wonder what to have for supper tonight. The matter seems of rather less importance now that I am the only one to eat. I reckon I'll just fix me a sandwich and call it a day.

A few tomato seeds hit the pages as I put down my meal long enough to find Benton's obituary. It was more of a moving tribute put together by some members of the church.

When the paper returns to its original fold, I notice that young man again—the one they say murdered that boy from up in the village down at the schoolhouse. There's a picture of him from his last yearbook, and there's a picture of another gentleman beside him who I first assume is his father. I examine the article further to find that it is a civil rights lawyer from Rock Hill, South Carolina, one Mr. Edmond Tillmore, Esquire. The trial had been postponed due to circumstances surrounding his legal representation but is now slated to proceed next month. The picture doesn't match the story at all. His bright young eyes could well be Benton's staring at me through the page.

The next headline down reads, SPIRE'S GROCERY SOLD TO CLARK ELLISON and I find myself unable to read any further. I've had enough for the day.

I switch off the kitchen light and head for a quick bath. I have to play at church tomorrow. Mostly I expect that I'll have a long prayer list tonight, and I'm ready to get to it.

20

HUNTER

Six months and I ain't used to bathing with other dudes or wearing shoes in the shower. Don't nobody pay attention to nobody else, but I miss taking my time. I miss that good soap my mama buys, my hair moisturizer, lotion, my scents . . . here you have a little box on the wall. You push a button and "cleanser" come out. You s'posed to use the same stuff on your head you use to wash your ass. It smells clean, I guess.

I know the guy in the shower next to me, Billy Ray. He's country as hell, but we get along good. He loves to sing that country twangy music when he showers. He must know a hundred thousand songs 'cause I ain't heard the same one twice. His accent threw me when I first met him, but he ain't nothing like them village boys. Made me think of what my dad used to say 'bout judging books by the cover. He used to say, "Son, if you paint every white, Southern person as a racist, you're doing the very thing you're accusing them of."

Time's up. Water turns off. Feel real cold until I get my towel and dry real good.

At least they let us get dressed by ourselves back in our cells. I can't wait to get out this jumpsuit they make us wear to and from the shower and get back in my regular sweats. They ain't fly, but they comfortable. Not bad to wear to pass time, and I got all kind of time.

Still, no matter how long I been in here, my mind comes back to the same night every day. Even putting on my shirt fast because it's cold puts me back at the house tryin' to get out of there fast to beat that dude's ass. Sometimes I feel bad I didn't wait for school or show my dad what happened, but those thoughts never even came up. I got that last Snapchat message from Scott talking 'bout, *We can go right now, boy? I'll meet you now. You pick the place. You got wheels ain'tcha? I seen it. Pretty nice car . . . for a coon . . .*

I don't know, man. It's like he finally found the right button or something. Like he been pressing all he could find and I been doing good about it, you know. But he finally found the one that put it to where there was no going back. I was so mad I couldn't even type. I sent him a snap, no filter, just me saying something like, *I gotchu. I gotchu! Right now, white boy, right now. School parking lot. No bullshit. Don't be bringing three, four dudes with you. Just you, me, fists. Right now.*

I snatched my sweatshirt, told Mama I was going to Addie's house, and set off straight for school. I got there first so I could be sure dude showed up alone. When he pulled in, I could see into his truck and it looked like he was by himself. I parked under one of the lights so he would know I came to face him myself, just me. No crowd, nowhere to hide, nobody to have my back. Just me.

He parked by a light pole two rows in front of me. He sat in his truck for a few minutes. Finally, I got out, he got out. I said, "Whatchu want, son? Whatchu tryin' to do?"

He comes back all country, "I'm here, boy. I told you I would meet you wherever, whenever!"

Just the way he talked made me mad. I mean I hate to talk bad about someone that has passed, but I hated that dude.

"I'm right here, white boy. I got all you want!"

He started walking up on me. I dropped one leg back to balance. I know my arms longer than his so I planned to get the first lick in try to break his nose and make it to where he can't see good. Man, I was ready too. I wanted a chance to get back for him surprising me the night we marched. I ain't get the chance to come back on him good. Them cops, and some that wasn't cops, was breaking us up and leaving their side be.

He kept coming, looking like he was about to break into a run or something. I remember thinking, *Good son, run yo' ass over here. All the better when you meet my fist. You'll be on pavement* . . .

He got halfway to me, but quick as he got under the light in the row between where he parked and where I was, *bam!* Dude dropped like a limp shoestring. I looked all around to see if I could figure out where the noise come from, but with the echo I couldn't tell. I couldn't tell if I should check on dude or get in my car 'fore somebody shoots me. Everything was so quiet and still that even my breath felt like it was too loud.

I took a few quick steps over by where he was laid out, but I couldn't see his face in the shadow. It didn't look like he was moving, but I had to check anyway.

I made it all the way there, knelt down, and tried to turn his head. It was all warm and wet. Dude's eyes was open. He must have been dead before he hit the ground.

I sort of backed up to my car, my eyes locked on what just happened. When I looked at my hands, they was dripping blood on my shoes. I tried to wipe them off on my shirt, but it just smeared it everywhere. That's when I heard the siren coming.

For a second I ain't know what to do. I locked myself in my car with my hands on the wheel. I thought about driving, but what good would it do?

I see the blue lights pull in and I froze. I don't remember nothing else 'til I woke up here.

"Mail call, McMillan." The jail trustee, who I don't trust, shoves my papers through the door. He's a prisoner too. Been here longer than me. I think he jealous that I get so much mail and don't nobody send him nothing.

I flip through what today brings me. Looks like Mama and Addie wrote me, and there's a copy of the newspaper out of Fayetteville. I can save the letters for later, so I can read them slow. The sound is louder than I thought it would be as I whip open the front page to see the headlines.

On the cover I see my face beside a picture of my new lawyer Addie's mom got me. She believes in me, just like Mama. His name is Mr. Tillmore. He's real nice. Told me to just call him Ed, but I prefer we keep business businesslike. I see he wrote to the editor about my case.

My client is not only held away from his family and without any mental counseling or regard for his personal well-being, he is also the victim of the unjust and willful targeting of both the sheriff and the mayor of Betterton. In response to my being retained, they dismissed Judge Leach, who had lawfully been assigned to handle this case when it came under adjudication. They proceeded to find and retain one of their racist cronies from Georgia where Mr. Inman was originally from and appointed him to the bench instead. His first act was to then deny our reasonable request for a change in venue due to the nature of the crime, the makeup of the town, and the unlikelihood of our having a fair trial.

Given the evidence, the lack of a weapon, and the nature of the fatal wound it is physically impossible for my client to have committed this awful crime. It is our position that he is, in fact, the second victim in this case. He, too, has had the life he knew taken from him. He sits caged like an animal at the mercy of the sheriff, the mayor, and the grieving but misguided McMillan family.

We acknowledge they are mourning, and we are exceptionally sorry for their loss. But keeping my client incarcerated when he is so blatantly and undeniably innocent will not bring their son back to life.

My client has been subject to hate mail, protests, and even harassment toward his family. These attacks have been racial in nature and threatening to say the least. We urge state police to look into the legal and ethical violations in this case immediately.

I read it back through a second time and try to process it a little slower. Mr. Tillmore sure does know how to write out how I feel. It's hard not to get down in here, man. I felt so hopeless until he came along. I ain't saying I'm going to walk, but at least I got a chance.

Addie's letter says she'll be at the trial, and Mom and Dad send love and prayers. I can hear my mama's voice as I read and my eyes well up so I can't see to finish what she wrote.

Looking out the window, I see a crow flying free. I can almost feel the air rushing over my face as I close my eyes and pretend I'm with him.

21

IRIS

Life's always done me hard. Daddy run off when I was two, got a job when I was ten to help Mama feed me and my brother Anthony, pregnant at sixteen, and married at seventeen without a pot to piss in or a window to throw it out of. We have worked hard for everything we got.

Hutch is with Beech and them having some big rally tonight at the mill, getting folks charged up before tomorrow's trial. I couldn't go. I been sitting in the porch swing sipping Jack Daniels and Coke, filling up that Folgers coffee can with cigarette butts.

The night is still, like even the trees don't know what way to move. The chains on the swing creek against the hooks they're hung on as if the damned thing is crying out the way I'd like to.

I got a few things to do around here, but it don't matter. Nothing really matters now that my baby's gone. I crush out my smoke and wash my last drag down with the last of my whiskey. I swirl the ice around in the bottom of the glass a few times before I get up.

The screen door slams behind me as I come in to wash up the supper dishes. About all I've been good for since Scott died is cleaning. I guess it's something to do that takes up time and attention. I ain't a mother no more. My husband is so beat up inside and lost without our son that he ain't interested in my duties as a wife. So, I clean. I cook, I clean, and I swing on the porch.

The hot water feels good on my hands, which are still cold from sitting outside. My mind jumps back to when Scott was just a baby. I'd wash his bottles three or four times each just for good measure. I washed him in the sink too. He'd giggle and smile up at me while I'm singing him my daddy's favorite Kitty Wells music. Everything was right with the world. Hutch'd come in, pinch my bottom, and plop down at the table. I'd dry the baby and lotion him up real good, put his diaper on, and hand him to his daddy. The two of them would keep me company 'til I'm finished making supper.

I clear the last of the dishes from the table and go back to washing. I never have minded cooking or cleaning. I felt like I's born to be a mama and a wife.

Back in Georgia me and my sister-in-law Jenny was pretty much the same person, just in different houses. Hutch and his brother would get into it about politics and worrying about blacks and immigrants. Me and Jenny never fooled with any of that mess. She had Trent, I had Scott and we all had each other. We focused on our boys and raising them up to be good people the best we knew how. We'd spend afternoons sitting in my yard or hers, smoking, talking about husbands and groceries, watching the kids run around and get dirty. Both the kids was close until high school. They sort of drifted off from one another just like their daddies done. But me and Jenny stayed thick as thieves. Why I ever agreed to leave is beyond me now . . . Shit!

Dammit! God, I forgot there was a knife under the soap. When the water clears the blood away from my finger so I can see where it is coming from, I can tell the cut ain't that bad. I wrap it up in a dry dishtowel and head down the hall to the bathroom for some ointment. I hate a finger cut. It's like whatever gotcha just pissed the nerves off without cuttin' 'em clean so they sting like hell. It's not so bad once the Band-Aid is on.

I let the water out of the sink and wash the bubbles down clean. I grab the glass I just washed, which ain't had time to really dry yet—still warm too. Couple of chunks of ice and me and Jack Daniels are together again . . . I hear Emmylou Harris singing in my head *Together, again* . . .

Tonight I'm in the mood for the baby book. Last night it was school annuals, but thinking about my angel baby makes me want to look through this. The white cover feels as smooth as satin in my hand, just like my Scott once was.

I grab me a blanket and go back outside to my swing, light up, and go back in time to when I meant something to somebody. I was Scott's world and he was mine. Hutch was along for the ride, and we got along okay for a couple glued together by a shotgun wedding and a baby boy. But I lived and breathed to raise my child.

I take a sip and listen out across the night air. I can hear the noise they're making at the mill, but I'm glad I don't have to take part. It'd be too much for me right now. Besides, I ain't all fired up and angry at that McMillan kid as they all are. Maybe I should be, but I ain't. Whatever his lawyer put in that Fayetteville newspaper really set 'em off.

I don't know if I'm doing any of this right. I should want someone to pay for what happened to my son. I should fly into an angry rage every time someone speaks his name or shows me a picture of him. I should be carrying a torch and screaming for a hanging down by the courthouse right now, but I'm not. I just feel empty and dead inside. Besides, what good would come from killing another mother's baby?

Scott smiling up at me from the page helps a little, but the tears blur him out. I wipe them clean and have another smile with him. I light up again and lay down on the porch swing to think. I don't want no protesters outside the courthouse tomorrow. Hell, I don't want no trial. Why should I have to relive the worst nightmare anyone can imagine over and over out in front of everybody?

They'll all be judging me too. Do I look sad enough? Am I dressed too nice or too homely? Do I cry at the right times? Do I look angry enough at the defendant or his family? Lord, it'll be hard enough getting through the whole experience without people looking me up and down the entire time. And what in God's name will I say or do if I have to be face to face with his mama?

I want to run. I want to get up from this hell hole and just take off not knowing or caring where I'm going . . . but I don't. I just curl up with my baby book under the blanket and fall asleep in the night air with the help of Jack Daniels and memories of my angel baby boy. The thought of not having to wake up tomorrow is more comforting than it ought to be.

22

ADDISON

I s this where this war has led us? I can see the protesters lining Main Street the moment we turn off of Old Mill Road. I can't help but wonder why these people have Hunter already tried, convicted, and condemned to the gallows before the first words of the trial are even spoken.

They look vicious, rabid even. Their expressions are so full of contempt that I try hard not to meet their eyes even though the windows of the SUV are heavily tinted.

Sharron, Mr. Tillmore, the McMillans, and I are riding together for consolation as much as solidarity. Sharron holds one of Ms. Alberta's hands, Mr. Tillmore the other. The smell of the leather mixes with her perfume, and the muffled sound of the engine and tires are oddly soothing given the situation. I exchange nervous, worried smiles with Mr. Sam as the vehicle comes to a stop at the base of the stairs at the courthouse.

I've never realized how tall this old building is before. Today, looking up at the eagle perched at the top gazing purposefully over Betterton, I find the height intimidating and halting.

I suppose the serious nature of the events, which are soon to unfold, are not lost on any strand of the town. The sounds of sharp voices bring my mind back into focus.

The angry mob of Eastenders yelling in protest is parted like the Red Sea by the state police who have been sent, not invited, to assist in maintaining the peace at such a time of unrest. I can hear them, but I don't even try to make out the words they are saying. I stare intently at the doors at the top of the slick, stone stairs as if my own salvation were just beyond the threshold.

The atmosphere inside the front entrance hall is altogether different. There are murmurs and hushed whispers, but not enough to muffle the sound of the old floorboards creaking under the now threadbare carpet. The musty smell in the air does little to calm the serious, almost somber, feeling that hangs in the air.

The tension is greater still when we reach the courtroom itself. The courtroom is not surprisingly divided into regular Betterton residents on the left and Eastenders on the right . . . both sides of the war keeping to their own. Looks are exchanged here and there, but little more. Sharron and I are seated behind the defense table as Mr. Tillmore takes his position on the other side of the short, wooden partition, which separates spectators from participants. He sits at the table, opens his case, and begins to organize his belongings in what seems to be a very organized way. A glance up to the right reveals two unfamiliar gentlemen who must be the prosecutors sent here from Cumberland. They look serious and experienced to me. They look to be far more relaxed and at home in this room than I currently feel.

In the gallery there are spectators from both sides, but there seem to be more townies than anyone else. The courtroom is not huge, but I would say about one hundred people made it in. No protesters, I gather, just interested onlookers. The jury box remains empty as Hunter has waived his right to a jury trial. He feared that a jury of *his peers* would be a roll of the dice at best. He had also hoped that Judge Stockman would be reasonable and decide the case based on the evidence and merits of what is presented by the prosecution. Beech, I mean Sheriff Bethune must have had similar thoughts. That is undoubtedly the reason why we now find ourselves facing his replacement.

Bethune has been making a number of bigger and brasher decisions lately. He is trying to promote financial incentive packages for other, I gather, like-minded people to move to Betterton, and more and more of the natives move away. Even the Spires sold their family's grocery store to someone in the village. I even heard he'd sent Jackson and Kitchens to round up undocumented farm workers and threaten Mr. Price and Mr. Fetter with arrest.

The call of "All rise" from Deputy Kitchens brings me sharply back into reality. His smug smile makes him look drunk with authority.

"The Honorable Judge Carlisle Gerrick presiding." Kitchens looks full of himself, basking in his newfound authority. I'd like to slap that stupid toothpick out of his mouth.

The judge, an older, larger man who seems comfortable in his position, begins to lay out how the proceedings will begin today.

"The matter currently under adjudication is a serious one, with potentially highly consequential implications. In my court clients will speak to attorneys, attorneys will speak when given permission to do so, and there will be no outbursts of any kind from the rest of the people in the courtroom. There will be no overt reactions or catcalls of any kind in my courtroom, or I shall clear it with only essential personnel remaining. At this time, please make sure all devices are turned completely off with the exception of the one reporter I have allowed in to take a few shots and objectively report to Fayetteville the day-to-day progress of the goings-on here.

"In this proceeding the accused has waived his right to a jury trial. Arguments will be presented, items will be entered into evidence to be properly examined by the court, and witnesses will be heard. Each side will have an opportunity to cross each witness. Deputy Kitchens, please bring in the defendant."

Hunter emerges through a door to the left of the defense table wearing handcuffs, shackles, and an orange suit. Mr. Tillmore is on his feet before he could even sit down. "Your Honor, where is my client's proper attire for court? It has long been regarded as highly prejudicial to present them to the court in a manner which implies that they are hardened, criminal thugs. We sent over proper clothes yesterday."

"Fair point. Sheriff, any explanation for this mix-up?"

"Yes, Your Honor. We didn't get that suit back from the laundry in time for today's proceedings. It will be ready for tomorrow's, I assure you, sir."

"It damned well better be. Is the prosecution prepared for their opening presentation at this time?"

The balding redheaded man with the glasses and the jacket stands up first.

> "Yes, Your Honor. I would like to begin by stating what are the indisputable, and in many cases, eyewitnessed facts of the case. It is a known fact, and we have digital records that we will be presenting into evidence regarding the ongoing feuds between the victim and the accused in which insults were exchanged and threats were issued. Further, we have multiple witnesses that place the defendant at the scene of the murder standing directly above the deceased within moments of the shot having been. We have tested the blood found on the accused's hands and clothing and identified the samples as having come from the victim. When confronted by the officer, Mr. McMillan resisted arrest."

"Objection. Mr. Burke began with facts but has segued into opinion. Whether or not my client resisted is still very much in dispute."

"Sustained. Proceed, Mr. Burke."

"Yes, Your Honor. We have witnesses that place Mr. McMillan mere feet from the body within a minute of his death. We also have character witnesses who will describe in detail how Mr. McMillan frequently had run-ins with the deceased at school. It is our contention that Mr. McMillan lured Scott Inman into a dark parking lot, killed him in cold blood, lingered a moment to savor what he had done, and did not make it out of the parking lot before Deputy Jackson arrived on the scene. Thank you, Your Honor."

Hunter is hanging his head low, Tillmore whispers something to him, pours him a glass of water, and hands him a legal pad and pencil. I manage to touch his shoulder, if only for a moment. He turned, smiled at all of us sitting behind him, then quickly redirected his attention to the matter at hand. There's a look in his eyes. I've seen it before, just a friendly smile and his kind eyes. But this time it seems more meaningful, I guess. Expectant and almost . . . inviting. I'm not quite sure how to take it, but I can't dwell on it at present.

Mr. Tillmore is just as matter-of-fact as the prosecutor had been, but he speaks with far more feeling and emotion. He really commands the full attention of everyone in the room.

"I would like to thank everyone for being here with us today on what I know is a difficult matter for all of us to confront. And I must say that I do agree with Mr. Burke on one aspect of his opening statement. I do believe this trial should be rooted in the facts of the case—the ones that may be convenient, and the ones which may be exculpatory and counter to the narrative the prosecution has begun to lay out. Here are the facts they omitted. First, we are dealing with a young man who, before being assaulted by Mr. Inman at what was supposed to be a peaceful protest gathering, had no prior violent history at all. Further, the victim was shot in the side of the head while approaching my client. It would be physically impossible for Mr. McMillan to have fired that shot. Further, neither Mr. McMillan nor any members of his household even own a firearm. The only weapon found at the scene was a knife Mr. Inman had concealed and had been evidently trying to retrieve when he was killed. To cap it all off, my client had no motive to kill Scott Inman. A few teenage disputes on social media hardly warrant lethal force with no monetary or social rewards pending. Your Honor, when it is all said and done here, it will be more than obvious that Hunter McMillan was indeed at the wrong place at the wrong time. But he simply could not have committed this crime. At this time we would like to ask that he be released on bond to the custody of his parents and be placed on house arrest at that location. We ask this to ensure his well-being and to protect him from other elements inside the incarceration facility."

"Request denied. The court will resume tomorrow morning at 10 a.m. I'll expect full legal briefs, an evidence log, and any other motions or other considerations submitted to me in writing in my chambers no later than 8 a.m. I do warn all, I have very little patience for tardiness. Court is adjourned."

The sound of the gavel snaps me back into reality. Mr. Sam looks more serious and resolute than he had been in the car. Sharron is worried, but she looks like she's in for a good fight. Ms. Alberta hugs me tightly, and I feel a tear brush my cheek. She says, "It's in God's and Mr. Tillmore's hands now." Hunter is escorted back through the door from whence he came. He looks over his shoulder at me and half smiles. Then, he is gone.

We march back through the protesters who seem even more energetic now than they had when we arrived, make a straight shot to the SUV, and we are on our way. On the radio we hear that Sheriff Bethune has arrested two farmers, Price and Fetter, for allegedly hiring foreign workers. Rumor is his next move is to muscle them out and try to take over the whole northern part of the town and make his way south, pressing all of us out. This trial could be his spark to do it, and the Eastenders know that.

I catch a glimpse at the resolve in Sharron's eyes and draw from it. I won't give up without a fight. Especially for Hunter. Maybe it has taken this awful ordeal to make me feel how much he means to me. He has never let me down before, not even once. Every time he does something I don't like, it turns out to be in my self-interest. He grounds me when I feel like flying off in a thousand different directions. He brings me peace when I am troubled and support when I am at odds with life. Mostly, he's the first person I can't wait to share good news with or get an opinion from. What a terrible time to come to the realization that you love someone.

Back in the SUV the tone is decidedly more hopeful. On the merits, the prosecutor's case looks weak. Mr. Tillmore laid out in no uncertain terms how Hunter could not possibly be guilty of murder. In what little light chatter and recounting of the day we do, the general consensus is that *if* the judge is objective, Hunter has a real shot here. No one articulates that Bethune handpicked the judge. No one dares ruin the first sense of hope we've had in weeks.

23

HUNTER

Feels good to be wearing church clothes instead of a jumpsuit or sweatpants. I may not look exactly on point, but it's a big improvement over yesterday. These dudes that are walking me into court today ain't even cuff me. Guess that might be *prejudicial* too. The lights are much brighter in these halls than they are at the jail. I feel like I got a spotlight on me.

When we reach the door to the courtroom, we gotta wait for the judge to read instructions then invite me in. I'm a little nervous, and my hands are all sweaty. My life is on the line.

The door opens and the little holding area fills up with light from the courtroom. I see Addie on the first row and smile, but not too much. Mr. Tillmore said too many smiles or smirks would make me look cocky to the judge. I'm just supposed to act like I'm worried for my life and sad that somebody killed Scott. I ain't never like that dude, but I can't let on now. Judge will see that soon enough when he's reading our texts and snaps.

Deputy Jackson is over by the door I come in, Kitchens acting like the bailiff. Bethune is sitting at the table behind the prosecution with Scott's mom and dad. That dude look mad, but mom look kinda out of it. Beech catch my eye, nods, then looks away. I just look down to the table like I'm reading something from Mr. Tillmore.

Prosecution has to go first. That redheaded dude Burke gets up and starts introducing his evidence log. Mr. Tillmore went over ours with me last night to be sure everything was right and nothing was missing.

Before he could get to the second piece he wanted to put into evidence, this tall blonde lady in a fine ass, but whoop-your-ass black suit, shouts, "Wait!" and get everybody's attention. She comes marching up the aisle like she owns the place. Jackson stepped over like he was going to cut her off, but she reached in her jacket and pulled out a badge bigger than his. He backed off. The judge was pissed!

Banging that gavel with all he had, and trying to talk over the noise. "Now see here! This is *my* court and I say who approaches my bench! *Here! Here! Here*! I say! *Order*! Who do you think you are?" The banging stops when the lady puts her badge on the judge's bench and asks to see him in chambers. He agrees and they take off.

Just like everybody else in the room, me and Tillmore ain't got a clue what's done happened. I looked over and dude for the prosecution turned to Sheriff and the Inmans and shrugged like he ain't know either. It all makes me nervous. My hands are all sweaty. I wipe them on my pants and look around at all the confused faces in the room. Some of them had been sad, others had looked pissed off, but now they all look like they trying to figure out what is going on.

We waited about five more minutes 'til the judge come back. He wipes his head with a little cloth from his pocket, straightens out his black robe, and sits back down. His voice is kinda shaky and mad all at the same time. I don't know what to make of it.

"Please be seated. Ladies and gentlemen, we will not be proceeding today as originally scheduled. I will need to see Mr. McMillan and his representatives in my chambers at this time.

Sheriff, I have some news which may interest you as well. If you and your deputies would be so kind as to hang around in the conference room, I'll be with you directly."

Damn, what they going to charge me with now? Conspiracy? Some federal crime? This can't be good.

We reach chambers and the judge asks me to take a seat in front of his desk alongside Mr. Tillmore. The room smells damp and musty like an old basement, but it's as neat as a pin. "Listen, son. There's been, well, there's been some new evidence I think you need to be aware of," the judge says. All I can think is if that new evidence is a gun tied to me, that shit was planted.

"Hello." The lady's voice caught me by surprise from a couch behind me. She comes toward me with some dude that looks like he eat raw eggs and protein shakes every breakfast, lunch and dinner.

"My name is Shannon Finley. I am a special agent for the Federal Bureau of Investigation; this is Bill Maddox, my partner. In investigating totally unrelated matters, we uncovered some extremely important information that has direct implications for your case."

I got time. All kind of damned time. I'm all ears.

"Well, part of my job is taking part in a task force specifically assigned to secretly monitor recognized and radicalized groups in America. We monitor their intercommunications, intercept plans, try to prevent terror attacks, maintain profiles of the big players, you get the idea. One of these organizations, the Ohio Christian Chapter of the Aryan Brotherhood, caught our attention when they demonstrated a larger-than-usual surge in online presence—membership drives, ads, literature distribution, paid bots to deliver misinformation online, you get the idea. Once they were on our radar, we started looking around their business dealings. Seems like they had started receiving huge influxes of cash here recently from somewhere in this area."

"So what does that have to do with my case?" I'm confused.

"Well, we subpoenaed their bank records and found that a shadow group called Friends of the Cause had been sending them funds regularly. Like sometimes ten thousand a week. When we traced down the origins of that group, it led us straight to the IP address of one Mr. Delbert Bethune."

"The sheriff? Our sheriff? Still, how does that change my case?"

"I'm getting there. After checking out Bethune, we discovered that he'd recently been elected to public office. We thought we might be dealing with campaign finance fraud, money laundering, and any number of other crimes. What's more is, he may not be the only one. We might have a RICO case right under our noses. So we got a FISA warrant to listen to his calls and plant a listening device in his office."

"And?"

"And listen." She sets this little black box on the judge's desk and mashes a button. A hissing sound, then I can hear them clear as a bell.

Kitchens: I hope this trial ain't a shit show. Kid hiring that darkie lawyer from South Carolina threw me a bit, but I think it'll be okay.

Beech: I ain't worried about the damned trial. Carlisle will be a friendly. I think we're okay there. Far as the money, we took in about 25k this month. I sent about 12 of that to the mill and the rest to our friends. We should be bringing in a good bit more than that next week. Especially if I can get around council with budget for next quarter. Of course, you'll both get a little kicker. Kitchens: Yeah, I went by the mill today. They've started re-doing some floors on the inside and some windows on the front.

Beech: Yeah, I saw that.

Jackson: What about the woman? That report about the picture she found?

Beech: Nobody knows about her but us, and it's going to stay that way. And watch what you talk about when we in this office.

Jackson: Look, Hutch is up my ass to ensure justice gets done here. The onliest way we gone do that is to get this conviction and move the hell back on to the real prize. And if Hutch ever seen what I seen, we'd have another murder to worry with.

Beech: Dammit, Eddie, we got this thing where we want it. Money's coming in, a little goes out here and there. We get what's rightfully ours, what we're damned entitled to. We're building a utopia here. The brotherhood can recruit and use us as a fine example of how to replicate and keep the crusade going. And no picture found on the phone of a dead retard is going to change that.

Click.

I am still a little confused, and agent kind of seem like she can tell.

"A few of my men and some with the state police have been pouring over the sheriff's office and the desks of the deputies all night. While we found a few papers and flash drives that we think will be helpful in the money scheme, we did manage to find the phone and the official complaint lodged by one Mrs. Sally Grist. In her description of events, she tells how a very dear friend had passed over the summer. She had only gotten around to going through most of his things recently. She had plugged in his phone and was looking through some of the things he'd been taking pics of to enjoy in his last remaining months. Seems like one picture stood out to her. She described it on paper, and we found it in the phone."

Benton. That dude took pictures of everything.

She goes on explaining, "It clearly shows a man standing between the diner and the bowling alley, directly across the street from the school parking lot, leaning over the hood of a truck with a rifle in his hand. The date and time stamp put this man at the scene of the crime with what we think is the murder weapon. We don't quite know who it is yet, but it's definitely not you."

"I said all along I ain't never shot no gun."

"Well, the sheriff and his men are in trouble for a lot more than just this case, let me assure you. They're facing federal charges they can't even process yet. I doubt you'll have to worry about ever running into them again. Anyway, we found the phone and we know it's not you in the pic. You think you might could take a look for me?"

"Sure, sure, I don't mind."

She showed the picture to me to see if I could help. I look, then look again. Hard.

It can't be. This has to be my mind messing with me. It just doesn't make no sense. A rush comes over me like a wave. I can't tell if I'm mad, in shock, or both. I blink a few times and then sort of stare at him. Something deep inside almost expects him to turn and stare back at me. Agent Finley interrupts me.

"Be careful, now. You need to be absolutely certain."

I am sure. There's no doubt in my mind who this is. I look up, swallow hard, and tell the agents the identity of the real shooter.

"Bill, take three armed state officers with you to the conference room. The judge will show you where it is. Take Mr. Bethune, Mr. Jackson, and Mr. Kitchens into custody. I'll be at the jail soon to question all three. Officer Johnson is waiting in the hall, Mr. McMillan. He will take you back to jail just long enough to collect your things and you'll be free to go for now."

I hear her making a call to a state policeman about bringing the one who should have been in jail all this time in for an interview, but I'm too stunned in the moment to let it settle in that my nightmare is over. I'm too stunned to say much more than *hey* and *thanks* to the state cop who drove me back to the jail. I just watched the town roll by through the window, happy to finally be free and have my name cleared.

Down at the jail I grab what few things I had with me, said a quick goodbye to Billy Ray, went through processing, and hit the front door. I ain't ever fell into my mama's arms like this. I got Daddy patting my shoulder so hard feel like he's beating me. Over Mama's shoulder I see Addie. She crying, I hope, out of happy tears. "I'll be right back, Mama."

I walk over to where she is standing with Ms. Sharron. I go in for my usual hug, but she stopped me. She puts her hands on my chest and looks at me like she was trying to see if it was still me after all this time. Then she closes her eyes and moves her lips to mine. I kiss her back for a second, then pull back. When I see her eyes, she looks as confused as I am. A moment goes by and she says, "I've missed you? Got plans tonight?"

Hell, I do now! We both smile and look into each other's eyes like it's the first time we really see *us* for the first time.

24

TRENT

I am in the backyard trying to catch a quick smoke when I hear the truck pull up around the front of the house. Hell, they're not supposed to be home yet. What happened?

Hutch is mad as fire when he comes inside the house. I make my way through the kitchen door and meet them in the den. Iris seems confused, Hutch is just pissed.

"What's going on?" I ask, a little afraid of what answer will come.

"Hell, we don't know!" Hutch yells at me, spit coming down his bottom lip. "They just came in, put the whole thing to a stop, and took that boy away. I don't think anybody knows! I just hope they ain't offering him some sweet deal to get out of paying for what he done to my son, I'll tell you that right now!"

Iris pours a drink and sits down on the couch. "Hutch, they'll tell us something when they know, baby. There isn't anything hollering and yelling can do to help right now." She takes a big swig and lets her breath out like she's been waiting for that all morning. Hutch acts like he doesn't hear her, goes through to the kitchen for a beer, and heads out the back door.

"Aunt Iris, I . . ." I don't know why I talked at all. I don't know what to say. I don't even know what to think.

"You what?" she says, running her hands through her hair.

I can feel my mouth moving, trying to make words, but nothing comes out. Before I have to come up with some bull to cover the silence, I see an SUV and a Betterton Patrol car pulling up. I wonder for a second what Jackson's face is going to look like when he gets out, but it isn't him. Some dude I don't recognize slams the door and comes up on the porch.

"Police!" he says in a loud voice as he's knocking on the door.

Iris looks agitated as she puts her glass on the table and opens the door.

"What are y'all doing here?" she asks, "I thought you'd be down at the courthouse trying to sort this all out. What do you want with us?"

"Not you, ma'am," says a mean-looking dude with a mustache as thick as I've ever seen. "Son, I'm afraid you'll need to come with me," he adds, looking me dead in the eye.

"Trent?" Iris asks, first to the officer, then to me. "Trent, what is this? What's going on?"

"I don't know, Aunt Iris, I don't know," I say the words, but she can tell I'm lying.

The noise must have reached Uncle H. as I hear the screen door slapping and footsteps headed this way.

"What the hell is this?" he yells, beer in hand.

"We need to speak to this young man, sir. I'm sorry, but you can't come with him," the officer says. He asks me to come to the porch and I do as I'm told, and he closes the door behind us.

He's putting handcuffs on me and reading me my rights as my aunt and uncle stare at me through the door window trying to figure out what is happening.

"Do you understand these rights as I have explained them to you?" he asks.

"Yes, sir," I say, kinda quiet. I hear the door open and Hutch talking as we walk to the car. I'm kinda thankful when the door slams and I can't hear him anymore. I can't bring myself to look up at him as we back down the driveway.

The cuffs hurt and make it hard to sit up straight in the car. It smells like coffee and Old Spice in here. They haven't told me what I'm being arrested for yet, but it's not like I don't know. I just think they didn't want to say what it was in front of Uncle H. and Aunt Iris. They'll find out quick enough. I'm sure they'll hate me forever. I guess it doesn't matter much. I'll probably never see them again. I suppose I can live with that.

The ride through town is too peaceful, like it doesn't match what is going on in real life. I see the trees and the houses going by. It feels like they are staring at me too—wondering what I did to end up in this car. A big bump in the road makes me lean over a little.

"What am I being arrested for?" I ask, though I'm not sure why.

"They'll explain all that down at the police station. My job is just to bring you down there."

Coming up on the front of the jail, I can see Addison and Hunter. I wonder if they'll be disgusted with me or if they'll ever know the gift I have given them. Especially him. I suppose I'll have to wait a while to figure that one out.

The sun is almost blinding as we get out of the car. As I take my first steps into the jail building, all I can smell is sweat and piss.

As soon as the door closes behind me, the mustached dude that brought me here takes my cuffs off from the back and puts them back on in front of me. Then she yells, "Male check-in!" It echoes loudly in this little, dark space. I can hear my heart and my breath as I wait a moment alone. I'm scared but not terrified. I mean I've been wondering how I would handle myself if the truth came out. Guess I'll see today.

This Smokey-the-Bear-looking cat comes in, and my lady cop goes away.

"Any knives, needles, weapons of any kind or anything that'll stick me in your pockets, socks, or clothes?" he asks. Normally

I'd have three or four smartass jokes to make, but I'm not stupid enough to try this dude. He looks like he could break me.

"No, sir."

Then, Smokey pats me down, first real light like he's checking for big stuff. Then, he takes both my shoes off, removes the laces, and checks my feet. Then his bear-like hands trace my leg from my ankles all the way to my manhood. Not comfortable.

After the pat down I go to this tall counter where a lady who looks like she don't stand up too much is waiting. She looks up at me like she's reading a stop sign—like I'm not even a human. No smile or *how are you?* Just cold eyes. She takes my right wrist, then forcefully grabs finger by finger and covers them all one by one in black ink. Each one gets rolled into a square on a piece of paper with my name on it, then she does likewise with my left.

Then Smokey escorts me to a wall with a small blue cloth hanging up. Picture time. *Snap*, turn right, *snap*, turn left, *snap*.

Then I get handed off to a guy who looks more like a meat butcher than a cop. He walks me through this loud-ass room filled with rows of plastic chairs and a few televisions on the wall. These guys are all in street clothes, but they look mean as shit.

I hear a loud, clanging sound. I turn and look behind me, and the back wall where I just came in from is lined with iron doors with small windows. Some dude was pointing at me and screaming, but I couldn't make out what he was saying. My eyes darted around to the other faces in those windows. They're looking too. I've never disliked being seen so much.

The butcher walks me over to a locked door, says something on his radio, and gets us buzzed through. We walk down a gray hallway, which other than the clopping of his shoes and the shuffling of my feet, is quiet as a funeral parlor. The lights are dim and it smells like sweat and cleanser. The floor is all shiny, but the walls are painted dull gray.

We pass under light after light until he finds the door of a little room with bright lights inside. He removes my cuffs, tells me to have a seat on one side of this shiny metal table, and asks me if I want a water or a coffee.

"Water please, sir. Thanks."

After what felt like an hour of me counting bricks on the wall and playing tic-tac-toe in my head with the tiles on the floor, the door finally bursts open and two suits come in—a white lady and a black dude. On a normal day I'd say the girl suit was hot, but I'm too scared of her to think that way now.

"Hello, Trent. My name is Special Agent Shannon Finley. This is my partner, Bill Maddox. We are here to ask you a few questions about what happened the night your cousin Scott was killed. Please be advised that you are still under arrest, so you can refuse our questions and request an attorney at any time. Also your Miranda rights are still in play here. We will be recording our conversation. Do you have any questions for me before we get started?"

"Nah, I'm good." Black dude hands me a water.

"All right. Well, first can you tell us where you were on the night Scott died?"

"Before or after I shot him?" No sense in dicking around. They know it was me. Lying don't help at this point. Anyway, hasn't Hunter sat in here long enough for what I did?

"You shot Scott?" she asks. She seems surprised I didn't put up a fight or anything. "Yes, ma'am. I shot him. I'm not happy about it. I wish there was another way, but there wasn't. There just was no other way." I hang my head a little, but I keep my shit together.

The lady in the suit says, "Okay. Well, I thought I'd have to work a little harder than that." She slides a shiny printout of a picture over the table toward me. Ah. That's how they know.

"Can you identify the person in this picture, Trent?" she asks, looking down at the floor like she knows what I'm going to say. For a split second I look up at her and let the question hang out there.

Then, "Yes, ma'am. That's me." She looks me in the eye like she's about to ask another question.

Then Billy boy over there pipes up.

"You want to tell us what happened?" No, jerkoff, I'm talking to the lady. I keep my focus on Agent Finley, and she's returning the favor.

"Scott and that Hunter guy had been getting into it for months at school, online. Even got in a fight one night when the town had a rally type thing. Scott didn't really like . . ." I hesitate for a moment and glance at Agent Maddox. He shrugged his shoulders and put up a hand like *no offense.*

"Scott didn't like black people. Or brown people or gay people for that matter. A lot of people up in the village feel that way." I open my water and take a sip. I don't feel nervous, but my throat is suddenly very dry.

"I take it you don't share those views?" she asks, looking like she really does want to know. She's being pretty nice, considering she knows she's talking to a dude who shot his cousin in the head.

"Nah, I mean, I guess I don't say anything to them or try to argue them down. It's just never been really important to me. I just figure if you're a nice girl or a cool guy then I don't really care about all that other stuff. My dad and my uncle used to fight a lot about it. I just ain't really one who likes to fight, you know?"

Jerkoff over there pipes up again. "For someone who doesn't care for a fight, you sure don't mind a murder." I look him dead in his eyes and let that dumbass comment lay out there for a minute.

"Shooting Scott was the hardest thing I have ever done. *Ever.* But I did not commit murder. I did *not.* I stopped a murder the only way I could." I don't realize how angry I sound or how loud I was until the room is still buzzing when I quit talking.

"Go on," Finley says calmly, pushing my water bottle toward me and pointing toward the chair I haven't noticed until now I've almost left. I take a deep breath and let it out slow, then I sit back down and try to word it all right.

"The last night I saw Scott we were in his room. He was smoking weed and going back and forth with this dude nonstop. At first it was really getting on my nerves, then it just started to piss me off. He was reading me comment after comment, insult after insult, threat after threat. I mean he looked like a man obsessed. Almost possessed. He had this . . . this fire in his eyes. And I promise you the whole house could have fallen around him and he would not have put that phone down." More water.

"I'm with you so far. You mind if I write while we talk?" asks Finley, though I'm not sure why if we are recording.

I nod my head, and go back to that awful night. "Well, I finally couldn't deal with it any more so I stole one of Aunt Iris's cigarettes and went outside. I went out and stood between Scott's truck and Uncle Hutch's. I'd just lit up when the front door came open. I thought I was busted so I crushed out my smoke. I was pissed off when I saw it was Scott. He came over to me and showed me a message from Hunter that said something like 'Right now, white boy. The time is now. School parking lot, just you and me.'"

"You mean Hunter was challenging Scott to a fight?" she asked.

"Not exactly. You see Scott sorta made the challenge on Facebook. *You pick the time and place and I'll take you on* or something like that. This was a Snap from Hunter making his choice known. I said, 'Scott, you ain't going are you? That's crazy? A fight alone at school? At night?' But he wouldn't listen to a thing I said. It was almost like he didn't even hear me—like his eyes couldn't even focus long enough to understand what I was trying to say. Then, he pulled his fishin' fillet knife out of holster, which I guess he had tucked in the back of his jeans. He said, exactly like this, 'I got something for that coon. He ain't walking away from this one. Not this time.'"

"He used the word *coon*?" she asks, like she's surprised. Hell, Scott used that word like most people use *and*.

"Yes, ma'am. I remember that very clearly," I insist.

"So you believe Scott intended to hurt Hunter?" she asks.

"No, ma'am. He meant to kill him. To kill him dead as a doornail." Maddox interrupts, "So why didn't you tell his parents?"

"Hutch and Iris ain't much good to the world when they catch a buzz. Hell, Hutch would have probably helped him out. Iris was asleep from the whiskey in the back bedroom."

Kinley this time. "So what did you do?"

"I tried to grab him and stop him, but he got in his truck and pulled out slow, I guess so the neighbors wouldn't wake up. I came inside, seen Hutch kinda drowsy in his chair, go back to my room for my huntin' rifle, then back outside. Hutch always leaves the keys in his vehicle, so I put it in neutral until I got it to the road, then I cranked it up, no lights, and headed over to the bowling alley parking lot."

"Why the bowling alley?" Kinsey sounds confused.

"Well, the bowling alley and the Finer Diner are sort of across the street from the school and right in front of the parking lot. I knew I'd have a view from there. As far as I could tell there wasn't anyone around. I knew in my gut what I had to do. I had to let Scott make his choice."

"Make his choice? What do you mean?" Agent Finley asks.

"I mean, I knew I wasn't going to let him murder Hunter. I just couldn't do that. I also knew that I couldn't shoot Scott unless I absolutely had to. If he pulled up and the fight was fair, I was going to let it be. If he pulled the knife on an unarmed dude, I was going to stop him. The choice was not mine to make. That was going to be all him."

"Then what?" Maddox asks, a little more nice like.

"I see Scott's truck and Hunter's car. For a minute nothing happens. Then, Hunter gets out, followed by Scott. I got out of my truck and found Scott in my sight. I was begging God please, please don't do it. But as he's walking toward Hunter, I see him reaching for the knife. I only had a split second to decide. I took him out. A single shot to the head. It was done before I could really process it. I heard a click and turned, but it was that slow guy from town. I didn't know if he'd seen anything or if he did if he could even explain it to anyone. I didn't know 'til just now he took my picture."

For the first time since I pulled the trigger I allow myself to feel it . . . to actually try to accept that I did kill Scott. He's dead, and I killed him. And I will pay for it for the rest of my life. I cover my head with my hands and start to cry. It's weird, though. I'm not shedding these tears for Scott. They're for me. He made his choice, but I only did what I had to.

I'm not sorry I saved Hunter. I'm not happy I killed Scott. I'm not happy that I'll be locked up for God knows how long. I just didn't see anywhere else to turn. My dad always fussed at me for being wishy-washy and not being decisive. The one time I do make a big choice, I end up here. The strangest part about it is, I don't know what I'd change if I had to live that night again.

"Son, you need to talk to a lawyer." Finally I agree with Billy boy over there. So does Agent Finley.

"Yes. Yes you do. Are there any relatives you want me to get in touch with?" I keep my head down and shake no.

"I will be back in a few minutes, okay? We'll talk. We will make sure you have a public defender, and we will talk. You were straight up with me, there may be something we can do to minimize the damage for you. Okay?"

I don't answer. I just keep my head down and my eyes clenched shut. The door slams, leaving me as alone as I have ever been.

I open my eyes as a sense of relief seems to relax my whole body. I'm not sure if it's because the wait is finally over, or if I'm just glad I don't have to decide what to do next. Either way, what's done is done, and now everybody knows. They may not understand why, but what happened in darkness that night is now very much seeing the light of day.

I think I'm most relieved that I don't have to go back to that house—to them. I don't have to keep lying to their faces and faking sympathy for their loss. They raised an animal, and he died like one. I'm sorry it has to be this way, but I've been over that night time and time again. I can't find another way to make things right. Now Iris is hammered every night just like Mom used to be, and Uncle H. just goes on and on about what a good man Scott would have become if that *boy hadn't snatched him from us.* Funny how being dead suddenly makes someone a better person.

I keep telling myself I played my cards the only way I could. I don't have to worry about figuring out what my next move is now. All I have to do now is wait and see what hand I get dealt next. I finish my water, crush the bottle, and stare at the clock on the wall. For the first time since I came here, I let myself wonder what my daddy would have done and if he'd be proud of me.

25

ADDISON

The look on Bethune's face on the front page immediately after his arrest is branded in my memory. The boastful bastard that thought he'd risen like a phoenix from the ashes is now a caged bird. The council saw to it that Brad is deputy again, and we have a special election coming up in two weeks for the offices of mayor and sheriff. It's just a formality, but it'll be nice when it's official. Mr. Teal has decided to retire, and he has endorsed Mr. Fetter for sheriff, and Coach Mercer is the only one running for mayor. It sort of feels like we are all anticipating vindication as well as restoration of the town we once and hopefully will again cherish.

Most of the Eastenders are gone, many having left within a week of their leader's demise. Most of the houses in the village are empty but pending action from the state police before they can be resold. Our soon-to-be-elected new leadership has been negotiating with a company from California to convert the mill into a plant that makes fiber optic cable. It seems we may see new, and this time welcome, life breathed back into this place.

The only remaining Eastender that I know by name is Iris Inman. Her husband left town like so many others, but she just hung around. She started working at the bowling alley, but she mostly keeps to herself. Every now and then I swear I meet her eyes at the store or the diner. She lets her gaze linger for a moment before going about her business. It's almost like she's trying to connect with me—to tell me something. I think she would love nothing more than to make friends here, laugh and joke with them, and find some sort of normal life after the awfulness she has been through. Maybe she can't figure out quite how. Perhaps she doesn't have the strength. So she's just here— just being.

Hunter and I have been virtually inseparable since his return. Mr. Sam and Mrs. Alberta have become even more like family to me. It's odd how such a devastating event can wind up bringing people closer together. In fact, Sharron and I are going over to their house for dinner tonight, but I have something to attend to first on this lovely September afternoon.

I love the fall, always have. It's not cold in North Carolina, but it's not warm enough for shorts anymore either. It's a good time to sit on the porch with a cup of pumpkin spice coffee and settle into a good book. It's nice to be able to do that again, now that the war is over. The hardness of Betterton has softened greatly in these last few weeks. It's like there's a peace in the air . . . like we are allowed to relax again. I can't today though. I have to go see Benton and update him on the latest happenings here in Betterton.

Mrs. Grist lets me pick a few of her last chrysanthemums from her garden to take with me. I invite her to go with me, but she simply smiles and says, "I don't need to go there to talk to Benton, sweetheart. He lives in my very soul. I find myself having conversations with him when I'm working in the garden or cooking one of his favorites. He walks with me everywhere I go." We embrace warmly, then exchange kindred smiles as I turn to go.

Sharron graciously gives me a lift over to Betterton Gardens. The ride is mostly quiet except for the music lightly coming from the radio. Mama is kind enough to wait in the car this time at my request. She knows fully that this is a conversation that is best shared just between me and Benton. I have been trying to find the words, the thoughts to express to him ever since his funeral, but articulating what I feel has been more difficult than I would have thought. I have decided that I can't really plan a speech or a poem. That would seem somehow unfitting. I have decided just to speak from my heart and speak to him as honestly as possible. Still, it may not prove an easy task to keep my composure.

The day is calm and still. I stand silently for a moment enjoying the tranquility of it all. A flock of birds breaks the serenity of the situation and prompts me onward.

Benton's stone is still shiny and new—ornate with angels and a beautiful cross in the center. I find it difficult to believe he's only been gone for such a short time. It seems I have been missing his smile for years. I lay the freshly picked flowers on his grave as a crow lands on a small, white mausoleum close by.

"Well, I've just come to say hello, my friend. Ms. Sally told me to send her love, and everyone at church is always talking about how much you're missed since you've been gone. I brought you these." I point to the flowers by the stone, a tear in my eye and reverence in my heart.

Benton was a kind soul; the sort of man I want my children to know and love. The kind of man I will want them to be like. He had all of the qualities that I feel make humanity all the more good at its core—decency, honesty, empathy, kindness. I guess I haven't realized until now how much we take the gentle people in life for granted. I could not have imagined what a vacancy would be left by his passing, but it's inescapable now. The very idea of his nature brings a warm, comforting wave over my body and a smile to my soul.

"You know, Hunter and I are quite the item now. I'm sure Sheriff Bethune would never approve, but luckily I won't find myself subject to his self-righteous blustering and ramblings anymore. You'll be quite pleased to hear that ole Beech, Kitchens, and Jackson are sitting at FCI Butner Low prison awaiting trial with the feds on multiple counts. I would be interested to see how their set of—I'll be kind and call them *beliefs*—work out for them on the yard of whatever correctional institution they eventually wind up calling home. People have been moving out of the Eastend and scattering like roaches when the lights are cut on. Like all vermin, most of them get away at night." A breeze ruffles the trees. I pretend it's Benton laughing, smiling down on me from heaven. The squawk of the bird helps me regain my purpose.

"Your picture saved Hunter, Benton. Your pictures always meant the world to you, now they mean the world to a whole lot of people. You're the hero, Benton. You made it right when nobody else could. I do beg of you please not to feel cross toward Trent. He did the right thing as best he could, Benton, I hope you know that. He saved Hunter's life that night whether he did it the right way or not. The only one who had really set out to commit murder was Scott."

It's the truth. I know in my heart that Trent did not want to kill anyone. He found himself in an impossible situation, and he had to make a very fast choice—one that, I might add, saved an innocent life. I have written to him once, but I have not received any correspondence from him at all. I wonder if he was simply content to disappear—to go and not be thought of.

The truth of the matter is that I think of him often. I wonder what he would be doing had he been able to go on with his life. Would he have stayed when the others fled in the aftermath? Could he have graduated and gone on to a happy life in another place? Would he and Hunter, in an odd twist of fate, somehow have become friends? I can't know—it feels so unfair.

The cruelty of the entire set of circumstances rushes back to me for a moment—I feel my cheeks flush with anger and my jaw tighten. The teachings of so many had led to the radicalization of the few. Fanaticism created a powder keg, and something as silly as a Facebook post is enough of a spark to shatter so many lives.

Why do people give in to the false comfort of ignorance so easily? Why do they find it harder to understand than to hate? Why do they not see that life can be so full and beautiful if we only look for the good in others? Benton saw that. Some people thought of him as not being very smart, but he understood quite clearly what many find impossible to grasp. The hardest of hearts can be smoothed by the smallest of smiles. Benton saw beauty in everyone, everything around him.

That's why he loved his pictures so much. I think when life, or the people in it, became harsh or ugly, he could just return to something beautiful he had captured in a picture and be happy again. I guess he had a lot to teach the rest of us all along.

I thought back to affection and my attention back to my late friend.

"Benton, I want you to know that you have taught everyone in this town so many, many wonderful lessons. That it never hurts to be kind to someone. That we should always check on a friend in need and try to bring joy to any situation. Most importantly you taught us that seeing the beauty in the world, seeing the good in people, is the most important thing we can learn to do. Every season brings God's beauty, every person has value, and all of us need love. You really knew how to see the grace in all things and nourish it with love. I don't know if you really hear me or if it's just me and the crow, but I love you, dear friend. I love you always."

A wind gently pets the flowers and dries the tear as it slowly descends my cheek. My lips form an almost involuntary smile as I nod slightly at this stone monument to the beautiful life that was. May he soar now high above us all.

I touch the cold stone, shed a single tear, and the crow takes flight.

Bonus Chapter

JACK

The warm summer air caresses my face as I make my escape, in broad daylight, from the restraints of the town from which I have so longed to be freed. I am not sure if my parents got me this car as a reward for finishing my senior year so well or because they felt guilty about what we had all been forced to endure this last year. Winter and spring ended with one classmate returning from prison only to have another take his place—one locked up and the other set free. I somewhat know how each of them feels.

The rush of the air over my ears is almost sexy, like the breath of a stranger touching my body for the first time. It lures me forward, irresistible like the call of a siren at sea. I can't even bring myself to turn on the radio for fear that it might chase away the sensation. My heart pounds harder and my soul seems lighter with every stripe of pavement which passes by. I have longed for this day since I can recall, and at last it has arrived. I must confess it is far more exhilarating than I could have possibly conceived. Even the cool sensation of the air beneath my legs as I shift to peel them away from the leather seat is somewhat seductive. I have never felt so alive.

It's impossible to explain what it is to walk through life as a gay boy in a small town in the south. How can one convey the burden of simultaneously feeling as if he were both living a life in which he found himself unable to step out of the scowl of a spotlight yet chronically unobserved? Not to mention baring the scars of being gay and Christian, black and white, loved and loathed. People say, "I love you" almost routinely, like it's an obligation. Every time the words fall on my ears, all I can think is, "How? You don't even know me."

I will tell them in time. I cannot let the wounds of the past blunt the sheer pleasure of the moment in which I find myself. I feel like a bird in flight, basking in the sun as I dive and soar without a worry in the world.

Mom and Dad wanted me to wait until fall to make my way to Asheville for school, but I never entertained the notion fully. I shot out of that town like a cannon the moment I had my diploma in my hand and transportation in my possession. I have taken out a lease on a small apartment near the middle of town, which I hope to share with a roommate from UNCA. It took most of my savings from the last three years to make the security deposit, but I know in my heart it will be worth it. This is my chance to come out of the shadows—to just be myself without the need to lower my voice or be self-conscious about how floppy my wrist is when I gesture. The awkward, shameful cloak that has covered me for the duration of my young adult years is melting away with every inch I can put between myself and Betterton.

I will not disguise myself in any way ever again. I left my parents a letter attempting to explain who I am and why I felt such a pressing need to depart the place of my childhood. I have probably missed a hundred calls and texts, but I cannot be sure. I haven't even considered checking my phone for the last sixty miles.

I suppose I might when I stop for gas. I can't stay on I140 W forever without refueling, but the time has not yet arrived for that. For now my thoughts are free to roam from college to work, freedom to responsibilities, friendships to sex. It's hard to process even a small part of it. Still, I shall try.

How I long to be a resident of the town described by my mother as *The San Francisco of the East*. I want to plunge right into the very heart of it. I fantasize about the people I will meet and the avenues we will travel together. I yearn to discuss art and music, life and culture, pasts and futures of others who are gay like me.

I gather that belonging is perhaps what I seek most in this venture. I suppose I don't feel like I have truly been a part of any place or group of people since I was a little boy. My parents are blessings, don't mistake me. But even the most friendly and loving circumstances were no match for the mortifying idea of coming out to the world. I feel as if I have been traveling alone in the world—left to fend for my own well-being. I have forged ahead unaccompanied on my quest to survive youth. Finally, I chance to consider, the solitary portion of the journey seems to be at an end.

The emotions inside me burst free in the form of a scream into the wind, "I win! You hear me? I wiiiiin!"

No more walking sheepishly through the hallways trying to stay out of the sight of bullies at school. No more listening mindlessly as my Sunday school class discusses the morality of same-sex relationships. No more wondering if there was enough money, prayer, or titties I could find on television or the internet to change me. All of those ghosts feel years away, even if they are only miles behind.

I won't live that way again, ever. Once was enough. I make a personal vow, here and now, that I will never feel ashamed again. I will be me, and if people don't like it, they can just piss off. I am finished caring about the sensitivities of others while disregarding my own needs and feelings.

And no more of that *Little Jack* shit. That name kept me a boy—I'm ready to be a man. I want to meet new people, network with other queers, and finally discover who I really am without the fear of condemnation and scorn. I think Asheville will prove to be the perfect place for my rebirth.

We visited the Biltmore Estate when I was thirteen. While I will say I found the main attraction thoroughly impressive, I must admit that it is not what left the biggest impression on me. There is another image deliciously burned into memory.

Mom, Dad, and I were sitting outside a little restaurant having lunch the day after we toured Biltmore. I was having a club sandwich, fries, and a soda. Suddenly, over my mother's shoulder, I spotted two men wearing denim shirts, sleeves rolled up, over T-shirts and khaki shorts. They were laughing and smiling as if they'd never had an unpleasant feeling in all their lives. As they approached I could see that they were holding hands, their fingers tightly interlaced. Just as they were close enough for me to closely examine the features of their faces, they stopped to look into a shop window. They pointed at something or other inside, placed their hands on one another's chests, and changed direction to backtrack and enter the building. I waited, almost unable to breathe, for them to reemerge as my father finished his hamburger. When they reappeared, with what I gathered was a piece of art wrapped in brown paper, they smiled at each other, then kissed passionately, right there on the sidewalk for the world to witness. At first, I looked around, half expecting the sky to shatter or someone to yell horrible things at them, but that was not to be. Part of me wanted to run up and introduce myself to the pair of them, and another part wanted to dive under the table and pretend I hadn't seen them at all. In the end, I took with me a glimmer of hope. There were others out there, just like me, who were living freely. Those two men showed me that there was a chance for me—that I was not ultimately doomed to live a life of embarrassment and shame.

Now I have the chance to return there—grown up and on my own. I want to study business and open a shop of my own.

Maybe the pair of lovebirds will pass me by yet again, who can say?

I can't afford full-time tuition just yet, but I will work and save all I can. I am hell bent on making my own way in this world without anyone else's opinions or cautionary words of wisdom. I will do this—just me. I will learn to live and love on my own. One day I may return to Betterton, but I will certainly not remotely resemble the fragile little boy they once knew. That time has passed. That boy is just a memory now.

Perhaps the last few years there did help to dislodge me from my lonely place in the shadows of town. Maybe seeing how the quiet people I have always known could survive such an onslaught of vile intruders and emerge stronger, wiser in the end. I guess even the darkest of days can generate a sincere admiration for even the tiniest flickers of light. The good people of Betterton may not be cosmopolitan, but at least I know that they certainly are, at their core, good people. They may not fully understand how to nurture people like me, but at least they are intolerant of the kind of hatred and misplaced anger the Eastenders brought to town.

My mind shifts back to the present as hunger pains remind me that I will have to stop for lunch soon. The sun is leaving its mark on my skin, and it feels utterly glorious.

In the end, I pray that people seek understanding of those who are different from them rather than giving way to fear and anger. We all have so much to learn from one another, good and bad. We all yearn to be loved for ourselves without the need to paint a more palatable portrait to present to the public.

I thank God for getting me through the past, and for the chance at a happy avenue into a future bright with anticipation and wonder. I smile, sure of myself and my purpose, as I leave one life for the next—all but engulfed in anticipation.